DR. YEN SIN:
THE MYSTERY OF THE GOLDEN SKULL

THE MYSTERY OF
THE GOLDEN SKULL

By Donald E. Keyhoe

ALTUS PRESS • 2016

CHAPTER 1
THE MAN WHO
DID NOT SLEEP

THE ROARING voice of the city had died away to a murmur. It was the hour when Manhattan slumbered. High up in a dark building near Fifth Avenue, a furtive figure sat at the window of an unlighted room, a pair of binoculars raised to his eyes. His pose had the instinctive stealth of the East, though the man on whom he was spying was almost two blocks away.

Suddenly a faint buzzing sounded in the phones which covered his ears. He bent his head, spoke into the mouthpiece strapped to his chest.

"Control, Group Two." His voice was strained, for he had been watching constantly for more than six nerve-racking hours.

"Observer Nine," came a muffled voice. "Neither Michael Traile nor Eric Gordon has left the building."

"I can see Traile," grated the man at the window, "but he has been alone for two hours."

"Gordon must be in some other room," muttered the second voice. "We've kept the place covered—"

"Resume position," curtly ordered the man in the darkened room. As he leaned over the sill, dim light from the street far below fell on the sallow features of a Eurasian.

He lifted the binoculars again, gazed out into the night. A deep blue had begun to tinge the blackness above the skyscrap-

His pierced body sagged, quivering, on the blade.

er canyons, but it was still two hours until dawn. Beyond an expanse of lower buildings, a tall structure loomed. The man trained his glasses on a yellow rectangle near the top and almost at his own level.

The powerful lenses bridged the intervening space, seemed

to bring that lighted window to within a few yards of him. He was looking into a large room, apparently intended for a den. But the furnishing was not complete, for the library table was littered with curios, books, and various objects. A huge packing box stood on the Persian rug which covered the floor.

A man was moving back and forth, emptying the box. He was very tall, and his lean face was tanned to the color of bronze. It was a keen face, and strong. The pleasant set of his lips relieved a hint of grimness about the jaw.

The hidden watcher swore to himself. This man Traile showed no sign of weariness, yet the reports proved he had not slept in thirty-one hours. The spy kept the glasses focused as the other man went back and forth from the box to the table. Traile seemed to be hunting for something.

With growing bewilderment, the spy saw the objects which appeared. Already the packing box had yielded a pair of foils, a violin, a jeweler's lathe, and several pieces of chemical apparatus. In quick succession, Traile produced a set of boxing gloves, three cameras of varying sizes, and a dozen pistols ranging from a small French derringer to a Colt .45 automatic. Books and a score of cartons and bundles followed. One carton was torn, and as Traile lifted it some theatrical make-up materials spilled to the floor. He tossed the things onto the table, turned and drew a leather-covered case from the packing box.

This was evidently the object of his search. He laid the case on a pedestal beside a big easy chair. Seating himself, he started to unsnap the buckles. Then he paused, and the spy saw a tired expression cross his tanned face. He stretched his long arms, sank back. For a moment the hidden observer thought he was going to sleep. But instead, Traile idly lighted a cigarette and looked out into the night.

Though he was two blocks away, the spy jerked back, for Traile's dark eyes, as seen through the glasses, appeared to be boring straight into him. The impression persisted as he forced himself to keep watching. Even at that distance, he could feel the power of that motionless figure.

A peculiar, far-off expression came into Traile's dark eyes. He seemed to be thinking intently. He finished the cigarette, lighted another, then picked up a newspaper from the arm of his chair. His movements were oddly lazy.

The spy gave a sigh of relief as that penetrating gaze was cut off. He laid down the binoculars, wiped his damp brow.

Several minutes passed.

HE WAS about to lift the glasses again when a queer signal buzzed in his phones. He hurriedly pressed a button at the base of the mouthpiece. There was a double click, then a calm, sibilant voice spoke in Chinese.

"Main Control. Summarize the latest reports on Michael Traile."

The words were in an obscure dialect. The Eurasian replied nervously in the same tongue.

"Personal observation transferred from Number Nine to Group Control at eight fifty-nine. At nine one, suspected apartment entered by Traile and unknown man. Obtained photograph of latter by telephoto camera with night lens."

"Very good," came the emotionless comment. "As I supposed,

it is one of the new secret stations for the Q-Unit operating against the Invisible Empire. Proceed."

"Unknown man left at ten seventeen. At ten forty-five Eric Gordon entered apartment, bringing small black box, probably a portable radio."

"What report from the observer detailed to Gordon?" inquired the unseen Chinese.

"Gordon came directly from laboratories of World Radio and Cables," answered the spy. "Observer Eight reports rumor of Government arrangement with the company for Gordon's service."

"Continue the report on Michael Traile," came the toneless command.

"Examined the black box, moved out of my range to the left. Returned in two minutes, conversed with Gordon until one o'clock. Gordon then disappeared, but Observer Nine reports he did not leave building. Believe he is in another room, sleeping. But there is something strange about the man Traile. He has not slept since Group Two took over observation."

There was a sound as of harshly indrawn breath.

"Impossible! He had already gone without sleep for the forty-eight hours he was observed by Group One. You must be mistaken."

"No, Master," said the spy, nervously. "I am certain. And there is another odd point. From the material he has unpacked, he must have a hundred hobbies."

"I am aware of that," the unseen Chinese answered curtly.

"But this other matter is vitally important. You are sure he is still awake?"

"Yes, I can see him clearly." The half-caste lifted the binoculars. "He has just put down the paper he was reading. He is smoking a cigarette… *Ai!* This is puzzling! A few minutes ago he seemed tired. Now he looks refreshed, as though he had slept for hours."

"There is only one explanation," said the other man rapidly. "The cigarette must contain some mysterious drug which enables him to do without sleep for long periods. Watch closely—what is he doing now?"

The spy carefully focused the glasses, gazed into the distant room.

"Master, you will think me mad—he has opened a case of child's toys!… He is standing up—he has gone out of my range—now he is coming back with the black box which Gordon brought…. He is connecting it with wires to a toy church…. He is looking at the clock in the church steeple."

"That is enough," interrupted the man he had called Master. "I think I understand now."

There was a long pause.

"An expert rifleman could easily kill him from this observation point," ventured the half-caste.

"The secret of that drug is more valuable to me than his death," came the emotionless answer. "Here are my orders." He spoke swiftly for a minute. "Report at once if he leaves at four o'clock."

The phones clicked twice. The spy looked down at the luminous hands of his wristwatch. It was ten minutes to four.

AS THE carton of make-up material spilled to the floor, Michael Traile glanced quickly toward the adjacent room. The sound had not awakened Eric. He could see the

young Southerner where he lay sprawled, half-dressed, on the only bed the "Q-Station" boasted. Eric's hair was rumpled, and even in sleep his face had a boyishly genial look. He was breathing deeply.

For an instant, as Traile picked up the scattered materials, a bitter light came into his eyes. If only he, too, could know that precious gift of sleep—could shut out everything for even one short hour. But Death was the only sleep he would ever know.

He turned back to the packing box, his thoughts still somber.

It had been twenty-seven years since that childhood injury which had made him a man apart. It had happened in India, where his parents were traveling. He had been only two years old, but he knew the story by heart. A skull fracture... a hasty operation by a Hindu surgeon... then the discovery that the man had damaged the lobe of the brain controlling the function of sleep. Sleepless nights and days when they feared that he would die... the Yogi who had trained him to relax his body completely, even though his mind would ever be awake. His strange boyhood back in the States... a day and a night tutor, to keep his wakeful brain occupied with one subject after another... a physical instructor to balance that strenuous mental life with games, exercise, sports.

Traile found the leather case he bad been seeking. He sat down, started to open it, then paused, realizing a sudden weariness. He stretched, relaxing his tall form to the utmost, then sat back and idly lighted a cigarette. For a few minutes he stared out into the night, through the bulletproof window.

If he were right, somewhere in the vastness of Manhattan was hidden the most dangerous man in the world—Dr. Yen Sin, malignant wizard of crime, and head of that unholy organization, the Invisible Empire. Traile's jaw hardened. The Yellow Doctor had escaped him in Washington, and now he would be fully on guard. But there was one advantage. Dr. Yen Sin would be looking for five Q-men—instead of one man connected with five Federal departments.

He lighted another cigarette; the tobacco helped him to relax. With his mind still on the Yellow Doctor, he opened his newspaper. For a week he had watched for something that would give a clue to Dr. Yen Sin's activities, if he were really in New York.

His restless eyes flicked over the headlines. A gang killing... a senator's speech, warning of the danger of inflation... a hint of sabotage in the sinking of a new submarine, on its trial runs before being delivered to the Navy... a murder trial... a rehash story on the week-old disappearance of John J. Meredith, prominent Wall Street figure, and a missing-persons item hooked up with it.

Traile's eyes narrowed thoughtfully as he read the last story. Two of the cases were believed murder, but the bodies had not been found. The police knew of no motives....

He put down the paper and turned quickly to the leather box. His bronzed face was now alert; all his tired expression had vanished during that brief "relax-period." He opened the case. At first glance, it appeared to be filled with toys, each one clipped separately to the canvas lining. There was a tiny church, with a clock in its steeple; a brass soldier, with a bayoneted rifle; a small model ship; a toy pistol hardly two inches long; and a score of other similar objects.

TRAILE STOOD up briskly, crossed the room and brought back a small black box. It was a special microwave radio, a new self-powered type, developed by World Radio and Cables. It was still switched on, but so far he had failed to hear the strange Chinese code which Eric and one of the company engineers had caught two nights ago.

He connected two wires with tiny binding posts at the back of the toy church. Like most of his collection of "miniaturia," the church was not what it seemed. It was a diminutive radio, with a sensitive directional indicator.

As he sat back, waiting, his eyes strayed over the things which cluttered the room. They were like monuments down the long

vista of sleepless years, even to the language books on the table. He had been a linguist at ten. At fifteen, his mind had been that of a mature man. Since then his life had been a constant seeking for new hobbies, new problems to ward off the desolation of endless nights. It was this which had accidentally led him into the web of the Yellow Doctor's criminal empire.

A faint hum from the toy church told him that the miniature tubes were warm. He glanced at the black box. The standard broadcast and licensed shortwave bands were tuned out. Anything which came in now would be from an unlicensed station, transmitting in the micro-frequencies no ordinary receiver would catch. He set the dials again at the point where the mysterious code had been heard. But there was only silence. He waited a minute or two, then stood up and moved restlessly about the den. It was not quite four. There would be a long, lonely stretch before Eric would awaken. He picked up a hobby magazine, rummaged through it.

Suddenly, from the room where Eric slept, a low-pitched

buzzer sounded. He hurried into the room, slid open a small panel which hid a special switchboard. There were several numbered sockets. A bulb was flashing over the symbol "Q-5," which was his designation when he was working with the Department of Justice. The line was a direct wire to the Bureau of Investigation, at Washington.

"Michael?" came a barked query as he plugged in the phone. He recognized the voice of Director John Glover.

"Right," he said. Back of him, Eric stirred.

"I've a lead on Doctor Yen Sin," Glover said hastily. "The son of Peter Courtland was stabbed to death half an hour ago at the entrance to my hotel. It was done by a Chinese who got away. Before he died, young Courtland gasped out something about his father and the Invisible Empire. He had just arrived from New York, and was evidently bringing me a message."

"You haven't notified your Manhattan office?"

"No, the State Department says you're in full charge of the Invisible Empire case."

"Give me fifteen minutes," said Traile swiftly. "Then phone Lexington Street to send two squads of agents to surround the Courtland place on Riverside Drive. Tell them to close in quietly. I'll fire a shot if I need help."

"Got it," barked Glover. He hung up, and Traile turned to find Eric Gordon dressing.

"What's up?" Eric asked eagerly.

Traile told him while he slipped off his smoking jacket and fastened a shoulder harness in place.

"You'd better take a gun, too," he advised, as he put on his coat. "If Courtland is mixed up with Doctor Yen Sin, we may run into anything."

ERIC WAS ready in less than a minute. He hurried after Traile as the taller man strode into the den. They were almost at the steel-backed door to the hall when a sharp *da-dit-da-dit* rasped from the micro-set. Traile snatched up a pencil and pad.

"Here—you can take code faster than I can! I'll check the direction."

Eric began a hasty scribble, but the code abruptly ended. There was a long buzz, then from the silence which followed came a sinister, toneless voice.

"Main Control. Interpreter, Group Six, stand by."

Traile went rigid. It was the voice of the Invisible Emperor!

"Holy smoke!" Eric said tensely. "It's Doctor Yen Sin!"

Traile motioned him to silence, for the Yellow Doctor was speaking again. This time the words were Chinese. After a few moments there was a pause.

"What did he say?" Eric exclaimed.

Traile wheeled to a wall map of Greater New York.

"He simply counted from one to ten in Shamo dialect. What was that first code?"

"X-three-D, repeated," said Eric.

"Probably the call number of this 'Group Six'," muttered Traile. He took up a ruler, looked at the hour hand of the tiny church-steeple clock. "The bearing is just about a hundred and sixty degrees."

"—eleven, twelve, thirteen," came the calm words of the Invisible Emperor. "Alternate two-five interval, Interpreter."

"Look!" said Eric excitedly. "Your bearing line goes within a block of Chinatown, between Pell Street and the East River."

Traile seized a strap from a bundle and swiftly fastened the micro-set to the miniature church.

"Come on," he said, thrusting the set under his arm. "We can take a cross-bearing on the way to the Courtland place, and trace the station later."

"Why not follow it now?" demanded Eric as they went into the hall.

Traile set a special lock on the steel-backed door.

"The Courtland lead is more important. We might be hours locating the transmitter, and even then they may be operating it by remote control."

CHAPTER 2
THE CORPSE WITH
THE TWISTED HEAD

THE ELEVATOR came up, and they descended to the first floor. The lobby was deserted except for the desk clerk and two drowsy bellhops.

"You're up early again, Mr. Scott," yawned the clerk. "Don't you ever sleep?"

"In the daytime," Traile replied tersely. He led the way to the garage at the rear of the apartment hotel, and in a few moments his car was rolling out into the night. Free of building interference, the micro-set brought the voice of Dr. Yen Sin to an audible note.

14

"—at one-minute intervals, Group Six," came the silken accents both he and Eric had grown to hate. A monotonous buzzing followed.

"Watch the indicator," Traile said as he turned westward.

"All Group Controls, attention!" the voice of the Invisible Emperor came with a sharpened note. "On suspicion of treachery, Female Agent Twenty-two is being removed—"

"No, no!" a woman screamed. "You can't do this—I haven't betrayed you!"

The words faded out with a moan. Eric whirled frantically.

"That was Sonya Damitri's voice! For God's sake, Michael, follow that bearing!"

Instead, Traile jammed his foot down on the throttle, sent the car racing across Sixth Avenue.

"Doctor Yen Sin forced her to trick you before! Don't fall for it again."

"But that yellow fiend's going to kill her!" Eric cried wildly. "She saved our lives that night—we've got to help her!"

"The whole thing is a plant," rapped Traile. "I was a fool not to see—"

The shriek of a police siren drowned the rest. Eric spun around.

"It's a prowl car." He clutched the strapped set. "I'm going to take these and ask them to help me find her!"

"Stay where you are," muttered Traile. He slowed as the police car drew alongside, then with a swift movement turned his spotlight handle. The beam fell on a dark and vicious face under a low-drawn police cap. Traile saw a bloody rip in the man's half-buttoned blue coat just in time.

The pseudo-do-policeman snarled an oath, and then the driver jerked the police car into Traile's path. Traile stood on the brakes, snatched at his .38.

"San hai!" yelled the dark man.

Three crouching figures leaped up in the rear of the prowl car. They were outside with the swiftness of rats. Traile fired pointblank. The first man went down with a screech. Traile threw the gears into reverse. A yellow face flashed through the spotlight beam. Eric's gun blasted around the right side of the windshield. The Chinese pitched over.

THE PROWL car roared backward as Traile reversed. The third Chinese sprang to its running board. Before Traile could fire, he leaped across and landed on the hood of the sedan. Eric lunged around his side of the windshield, gun leveled.

A stream of dark vapor shot from a pear-shaped bulb in the hand of the yellow assassin. Eric's finger tightened convulsively on the trigger as he slumped back. His gun roared, spurted red flame. The Chinese gave a gurgling cry and toppled down against the windshield.

As Eric sagged back, a cold fury swept over Traile. He whipped the .38 toward the prowl car. Two shots crashed, and the man with the bloody coat fell limply over the door. The driver cut his wheels with a desperate speed. As the two machines scraped together, he twisted hastily in his seat. The ringed snout of a silenced gun poked across at Traile.

Traile's shot and the jump of the silenced weapon were simultaneous. A bullet ripped the seat cushion near Traile's shoulder. Then the prowl car raked past with a dead man at its wheel.

Above the scraping of fenders, as the cars pulled free, came the trill of a whistle. It was echoed by another not far off, then a siren wailed out in the night. Traile braked to turn, sent the car charging ahead. Those might be real police, or they might be more of the Yellow Doctor's agents. He took the next corner on two wheels, rolling the dead Chinese into the street. Without slowing, he switched off his lights, plunged into the first alley he saw.

As the whistle blasts faded away, he stopped, anxiously bent over Eric. With relief, he felt the other man move. He quickly propped him up at the window. Eric began to breathe more normally, and in a few moments he opened his eyes. He tried to sit up.

"Take it easy, old man," said Traile. "You'll be all right in a minute."

"What happened?" Eric asked dazedly.

"That killer sprayed you with some kind of anesthetic. They must have had orders to take us alive."

"I remember now," Eric mumbled. "It smelled like incense, then everything turned black."

"I was afraid at first he'd killed you," Traile said grimly. "Thank Heaven the Yellow Doctor overplayed his hand and gave me warning. But we'd better get out of this area in case he has others looking for us."

He started the car, and they emerged cautiously from the alley. He switched on the lights, zigzagged through the Fifties, and swung into Broadway at Fifty-seventh Street. By this time Eric had almost recovered.

"How'd you know they were fake cops?" he asked huskily.

"I wasn't sure," said Traile. "But it was obvious he wanted us to follow that bearing into a trap of some kind. When the police car appeared so quickly, I had a hunch they were Yen Sin's killers."

"Then they must've bumped off the real cops to get their uniforms and the car," said Eric.

Traile's bronzed face was hard.

"Undoubtedly. I saw a bloody knife-slit in one man's coat. And the blood was fresh, so this thing must have been very recently planned."

"But I still don't see," said Eric, "how Yen Sin knew you'd be tuned in to catch those messages."

TRAILE GAZED thoughtfully ahead as the sedan crossed Columbus Circle. "There's only one answer. He's spotted that Q-station. I was evidently being watched from somewhere—

unless Doctor Yen Sin learned through someone at the company that we were going to listen in for that code."

"I never spilled a word," Eric said indignantly. "And I sneaked out the set without anybody seeing me."

"Then the first idea must be right. It's clear that the messages were designed to lead us into a trap. From the way those last signals faded, they were obviously using a narrow beam pointed straight at the building. If it hadn't been for Glover's call, I'd probably have followed that lead—at least until Yen Sin brought Sonya into it. That was plainly intended to bring you racing to help her. And he knew I wouldn't let you go alone."

"I still can't believe she did it on purpose," Eric said miserably.

Traile slowly shook his head.

"You'll save yourself many heartaches if you forget her, Eric. Even though she's an unwilling agent, remember she's still in his power. Yen Sin holds her father prisoner at his base in China, ready to torture him—or kill him if she should betray him."

Iris struck at Traile's elbow as
the three Gray Men came in.

A stricken look filled Eric's boyish face.

"Then you checked on her story?" he asked in a low tone.

Traile glanced at the dash clock, increased the car's speed.

"Yes, through a source in Shanghai. Her father is Grand

Duke Sergius Damitri—one of the old Czarist regime. When the Revolution broke out, he fled with Sonya and her mother. They tried to reach Spain—Sonya's mother was Spanish—but they couldn't get out of the Orient. The Grand Duke became mixed up in espionage. His wife died, and Sonya was practi-

21

cally brought up to become an agent for the White Russians. Then a year ago Doctor Yen Sin drew her father into his web, held him as a hostage, and since then has forced her to act as a spy for the Invisible Empire."

Eric's blue eyes blazed.

"The damned fiend! To think of his having a white woman in his power!"

"She's only one of hundreds. Iris Vaughan is another example. He enslaved her through opium, so he'd have a spy in the British Embassy at Washington."

"Too bad the Embassy protected her after the raid on Yen Sin's hideout," said Eric. "She might have told plenty."

The sedan reached Seventy-second Street. Traile slowed, turned toward Riverside Drive, speeded up again.

"She was to be turned over to us next day, but she escaped that night," he said with a trace of glumness. "I thought we were clever when we managed to trace her to San Francisco. I know now that Yen Sin had her lead us there so we'd think he had fled to the Coast. And then she vanished right under my nose."

"Anyway, it did some good," Eric pointed out. "We linked our San Francisco communications with the other Q-stations."

"Thanks to your work," assented Traile. He turned northward into the drive which paralleled the Hudson. A faint grayness had come into the sky, against which the rows of towering apartments, broken by an occasional mansion, bulked in dark silhouette.

"We're almost there," Eric said quickly, as Traile leaned out around the windshield.

"Yes, I know." A sharp alertness had come into the taller man's face. "I was looking to see if by chance the D.J. cars had beat us to the place."

"You really think Courtland is working with Doctor Yen Sin?" exclaimed Eric.

"Not willingly. But the Yellow Doctor may have found some shady spot in old Courtland's life. In that event, he'll be a potential enemy."

A moment later, the car swung in toward the entrance of the Courtland place, which comprised one whole square block. Suddenly, Traile put on the brakes. The huge gates were open, but there in the center and barring the way was a shining crimson pole. In the headlights it was the color of blood.

"Good Lord!" Traile whispered. He leaped out.

"What is it?" Eric gasped as he caught up.

"It's a Chinese funeral pole!" Traile said tensely. "I'm afraid we're going to be too late."

He raced up the curving drive with Eric close at his heels. No lights shone from the mansion. He ran up the steps. The door was open, and from somewhere beyond there came an eerie will-o'-the-wisp glow. The silence all but shrieked.

Traile tiptoed to the doorway through which the flickering light showed. It led to a drawing room. He took one step inside, then halted, appalled, with Eric gazing white-faced past his shoulder.

Two yellow Chinese candles shone down from the head of

an open coffin directly before them. An icy shudder went over Traile. He was looking down on the back of a corpse—but the dead man's face was staring upward!

With horror, Traile saw the bloodstains which had dyed the man's white collar. Peter Courtland had been decapitated, and his head sewn on again—backward!

CHAPTER 3
THE GOLDEN SKULL

ERIC TURNED away, sickened, as Traile stepped closer to stare in amazement. Just beyond the candles, on a stand beneath a mirror, a queer bright object was gleaming. Leering down at the pale dead face below was a small golden skull.

Eric gazed blankly at it, but Traile's dark eyes suddenly filled with consternation.

"My God! The *Chuen Gin Lou!*"

"What do you mean?" Eric asked thickly.

"The Circle of the Golden Skull—one of the oldest, most dreaded secret societies of China. It's supposed to have died out. Doctor Yen Sin must have revived it, made it part of the Invisible Empire."

Eric looked back at the dead man and shivered.

"It's horrible enough, murdering him, but to sew on his head that way—"

"It's part of their ritual, based on the Chinese penal code," said Traile, as Eric broke off. "When a Chinese criminal is beheaded, it is the custom to sew his head on backward before giving the body to his relatives. Courtland must have been about to betray Yen Sin. This thing has been staged as a warning to others in the Empire."

Eric gripped his gun, peered around into the shadows.

"It's like a tomb," he whispered. "I wonder if they killed all the servants, too."

"We'll search the place as soon as those agents arrive," Traile answered. His eyes had hardly left the golden skull. There was a curious fascination about it. It had been molded by a master hand, and with diabolical artistry. Its proportions were perfect, though it was less than half the size of a human skull. In the flickering candlelight, a mocking grin seemed to play across its hideous metal face. Eric looked at it, startled.

"Lord! For a second, I thought it was moving!"

"It's only the light," said Traile. He thrust out his hand as Eric came closer. "Don't touch it. There may be some solid basis for that old fantastic story."

Eric stared at him.

"What story?"

Traile hesitated before he answered.

"The *Chuen Gin Lou* is said to have been a mysterious murder cult ruled by a golden skull. The skull was supposed to have the power of death. Only the members ever knew the truth, but there are well-educated Chinese who still believe that 'He who looks upon the Golden Skull must either kill or die.'"

Eric's jaw dropped.

"Don't tell me you believe that!"

Traile's dark eyes were somber.

"Eric, I've seen strange things in the East. I am not easily affected, but there is something about that skull—"

He stopped, glanced quickly at his watch.

"Those D.J. agents should be here in a few minutes. You know Bill Allen, and he'll probably be in charge. I wish you'd meet him—tell him to hurry in here. I'll examine Courtland's body, meanwhile."

Eric grimaced.

"You're welcome to that part. I'll be glad to get out of here."

As he went out, Traile stooped over the dead man. The beheading had been done by a skilled hand, for the cut was straight. The bloodstained stitches also gave evidence of surgical knowledge. Traile's lips tightened. Unless he was badly mistaken, this was the work of the Yellow Doctor himself.

He holstered his automatic, started to search Courtland's pockets. He did it cautiously, knowing Yen Sin's predilection for setting deathtraps in unlikely places. The dead man's pockets were empty. Traile turned, was bending over the golden skull when he heard something from the left side of the house. It grew swiftly into the sound of a woman's footsteps, a woman who was running desperately, fearfully.

Traile stepped back quickly into the shadows, took a hasty glance about him. The nearest concealment was a large urn on a taboret. He crouched behind it. The next instant a girl darted in from a door at the side. With a start, Traile recognized the pretty face of the blond English girl, Iris Vaughan.

Her head was bare, and her bright hair shone in the light of the candles. She halted for a moment, cast a fearful look about the room. From the half-opened bag on her arm she had taken a small, pearl-handled pistol.

She gasped as she saw the coffin and its terrible occupant. For a second, Traile thought she would faint. But the desperate light came back into her eyes, and she forced herself to go on. With her gaze averted, she passed the dead man's bier. She had reached the stand under the mirror when Traile silently moved from behind the urn. He kept to one side, so that she would not see his reflection. He was within a few feet of her, the thick rug muffling his step, when she suddenly turned. All the color went out of her face.

"Michael Traile!" she moaned. She stood as though paralyzed, then with a frantic motion tried to snatch up the gun she had laid down. Traile's long fingers closed on the weapon. He calmly dropped it into his pocket. The girl shrank back with a little cry. Traile's dark eyes searched her frightened face.

"So the Doctor didn't intend the Golden Skull to be left here."

She tried to speak, made a helpless gesture. Traile looked down at the gruesome figure of Peter Courtland.

"Once before, I told you there was no diplomatic immunity for murder."

"I had nothing to do with it," she said wildly. "I never even knew!"

"Then why are you here?" Traile interrupted.

"*He* sent me—" the words broke in a sob. "Please let me go—I swear I knew nothing of this awful murder!"

Traile eyed her sternly.

"Where is Doctor Yen Sin hidden?"

"I don't know!" she whispered. "All my orders come indirect-ly—"

"You're lying," said Traile, but part of the sternness went out of his face. She was dangerous, yet there was something pitiful about her.

He hesitated. "If you will give me the information I need, I'll see that you are protected against his vengeance."

"You're mad!" she cried. "Nothing could save me! In God's name, give me the skull—let me go—"

"What is its secret?" Trail demanded.

Iris Vaughan turned deathly pale. "I can't tell you—I don't know!"

"Perhaps you would rather tell the police," Traile said calmly.

With a trembling hand, she took something from the vanity bag on her arm. He reached out quickly, thinking it was another weapon. To his astonishment, she opened a jeweler's box and an enormous oval-shaped diamond blazed up at him. "Here!" she said tensely. "This is worth a thousand times the gold in that skull. Take it!"

Traile stared down at the shimmering jewel.

"The Vare Diamond!"

"It's not stolen, if that's what you're thinking," she said in a breathless whisper. "But it's yours—in exchange for the skull."

"I'm sorry." Traile lifted his head as the sound of hastily applied brakes came from outside. "But you have one last chance to talk, before the Department of Justice men get here."

She caught at him with frantic hands.

"Please don't let them take me!"

He could feel the warmth of her body as she clung to him. He looked down, steeling himself against the passionate appeal in her upturned face. For an instant, her very soul seemed to be in her eyes.

"Save me!" she whispered. "I promise I shall not forget!"

HE REACHED up to disentangle her arms. Outside, another car stopped with tires squealing. Iris moved back despairingly as a thud of feet sounded from the reception hall. But suddenly a wild hope flashed into her eyes.

Traile shot a look at the mirror. A bulky figure had plunged into the room. In that split second, he saw a strange gray face. Then he dived headlong back of the coffin.

The silenced gun he had seen gave a muffled *clunk.* The slug tore through the coffin, and wood splintered three inches above his head. He rolled over, came up with his .38 blasting. The other man jumped back, gun arm dangling. He made a vain attempt to shift the weapon and reload.

"Drop it!" clipped Traile.

The man's queer gray face jerked spasmodically, and the silenced gun slipped from his fingers. His eyes, small and deep-sunken, never moved from Traile. Hoarse voices abruptly were audible, then a French window to the conservatory burst open. Traile half-wheeled, expecting to see Bill Allen's agents. But to his dismay, he was looking on three more gray-faced men.

As the three leaped into the drawing room, Iris struck at Traile's elbow. The .38 roared, drilled a hole in the wall. Its

crashing report was followed by the ominous click of another silenced pistol. The mirror back of Traile shattered into a thousand fragments. He flung a swift-aimed shot at the first of the trio of Gray Men.

The man screamed hoarsely, stumbled and fell in a heap. Traile hurled himself toward the coffin as the other two leveled their guns. A sweep of his hand, and the candles went to the floor. In the darkness he heard a venomous hiss of lead from the raiders' pistols.

From the direction of Riverside Drive, an exhaust whistle throbbed four times. Instantly, a beam of light swept the lawn beyond the veranda. A fifth Gray Man dashed into the room.

"Come on!" he rasped. "They're surrounding the place."

"But the Golden Skull!" snarled another voice. "We haven't found it."

"I have it!" came the panicky voice of Iris Vaughan. "But we'll never escape now."

Traile leaped toward her as she started to run to the window. By the faint light from the shifting searchlight of the D.J. men, he saw the gleam of gold. He tore the skull from her hands, whirled toward the urn. In the shadows back of him, Iris gave a scream.

"It's gone! Someone—"

A crash of gunfire drowned her cry. The shots came from behind the mansion. Two of the Gray Men were silhouetted as they hastily picked up their dead comrade, carried him through the French window. Traile had barely placed the skull inside the urn and wheeled to the hall doorway when a flashlight probed through the dark. The man he had wounded snarled an alarm. Bullets plunked into the doorframe as Traile charged into the hall.

He dodged through the library, hurriedly opened a window, and dropped to the ground outside. A powerful spotlight in the hands of an agent covered him at once.

"Get 'em up!" the man ordered sharply.

"Hold it, Johnson," snapped another voice. The lanky form of Bill Allen appeared, with Eric close behind.

"They're getting away on the other side," Traile said hastily, as Allen recognized him. Even as he spoke, there was another burst of shots. He and the others sprinted around the front of the mansion. A big car was racing down the exit drive. It swerved suddenly, charged across the lawn and plunged through the hedge which bordered the yard. Behind it came a second machine, engine roaring. It whirled through the beam of an agent's searchlight, and for a moment Traile saw the terrified face of Iris Vaughan, where she cringed down by one of the Gray Men.

BILL ALLEN had raised a tommy gun for a burst at the car. At sight of the girl, he swore and pointed the weapon lower. A stuttering blast ripped at the wheels, but the bullets missed the tires. At furious speed, the car tore through the break in the hedge and was swallowed up in the gloom. Down near the main entrance to the estate, a D.J. car roared away in hot pursuit.

Traile swung quickly to Bill Allen, as several D.J. men ran toward the senior agent.

"The police will be here in a few minutes. I want them to

think that Eric and I are agents of yours—that we arrived here at the same time you did. Here's your story: You had a tip from Washington, dashed out here, and ran into a fight with some gangsters who got away."

"That bird I saw with the girl didn't look like any gangster," Bill Allen muttered. "He looked like a corpse."

"You'll find a real one inside," Traile said grimly. "But pass that word to your men, and then have them search the place. I've something to show you."

Allen gave hasty instructions to his men, and they scattered to search the mansion. Traile had drawn Eric aside.

"You recognized her?" he said in an undertone.

Eric nodded, his blue eyes still wide with excitement.

"Sure, it was Iris Vaughan—but where on earth were she and those—"

"I'll explain in a minute. But don't tell anyone but Allen that we know who she was."

Bill Allen strode back and joined them.

"Now, would you mind telling me what the hell—"

"Come on," Traile cut in. "We've no time to waste."

He led the way to the drawing room, tersely explaining what had happened. The lights were on, and one of the agents was just starting on to the conservatory, after an amazed stare at Courtland's body. Traile waited till he had gone, then retrieved the golden skull from the urn, while Allen gingerly examined the dead man.

"I don't want the police to know about this skull," Traile said rapidly. "It must have some tremendous importance. The Gray

Men were sent here to recover it. Not only that, the Vaughan girl offered me the Vare Diamond in exchange."

Bill Allen gaped at him.

"The Vare Diamond! Why, that stone's worth a third of a million if it's worth a penny."

"I know that." Traile scanned the floor near the coffin. "I thought she dropped it, but she evidently found it again."

Eric pointed to a pool of blood nearer the opened window.

"You must've finished one of those Gray Men, all right."

Traile's tanned face was flinty.

"If he'd been a better shot, I'd be stretched out here with poor old Courtland."

Allen shook his head bewilderedly.

"I thought you were screwy tonight, when I got Glover's order and you told me about Doctor Yen Sin and the Invisible Empire. But after this—"

"This is only a hint of Yen Sin's diabolical methods," interrupted Traile. "We're likely to have more than a hint when he finds we have the skull."

All three gazed at the golden object for a second.

"I can't see what anybody'd want of that thing," grated Bill Allen. "Unless it were to melt it down—"

"And tonight's work proves it's not that," rapped Traile. He lit a cigarette, took a turn back and forth. "From all the rumors and stories about it, the Golden Skull must be a sacred symbol. If you knew Chinese superstition, you'd understand Doctor Yen Sin's desperate efforts to regain possession of it. Millions of Chinese blindly worship lesser things than this."

Dr. Yen Sin sat before the talking Buddha.

"Then why did they leave it here?" asked Eric, puzzled.

Traile frowned down at the skull. "It may have been used in the ritual. The red funeral pole bears that out; it means, literally, that 'a man lies in a coffin within this house.' But someone must have left the skull by mistake."

A whine of sirens announced the approach of the police.

"Eric, you and I had better slip outside," Traile said quickly. "We want to be as inconspicuous as possible while the police investigate this."

35

As they were hurrying out with Bill Allen, one of the D.J. agents came downstairs.

"No sign of anybody up there, sir," he told the senior agent. "And Johnson reports the servants' quarters deserted."

"The servants have probably been kidnapped," Traile said as they reached the main entrance. "If I know the Yellow Doctor, they won't be seen again."

"By Heaven, he can't get away with this!" said Allen angrily.

A police car had come to a halt before the funeral pole and a strongly Irish voice was heard in a profane outburst.

"At least they're real cops," Traile muttered. He hid the golden skull under his coat. "Explain things as fast as you can, Bill. Eric and I will stay back with your men until you've arranged it so we can leave."

"I'll do my best," said the lanky agent.

But it was almost an hour before he could finish explaining to the satisfaction of the homicide squad. By this time police and reporters were swarming over the place, and a crowd had gathered at the gates.

Several of the D.J. men grouped themselves about Traile as he went out to his car, and the bulge under his coat apparently passed unnoticed. Bill Allen climbed into the rear of Traile's car, with two agents armed with tommy guns. Two machines filled with the rest of the D.J. men formed a close escort in the dash for Lexington Avenue.

Traile drove as fast as he dared through the early morning traffic. His bronzed face was stonily set, and his dark eyes flicked ceaselessly from right to left at each new intersection. By now,

Yen Sin would undoubtedly know the truth. There probably had been spies in that crowd back at the mansion. But there seemed to be no one following, and it would be difficult for anyone to pick them up on the zigzag route he was taking.

On the front seat between him and Eric reposed the mysterious, gleaming skull. Eric kept looking down at it with a morbid fascination. Suddenly he stared across at Traile's hard-set face.

"Michael, you remember what you said: 'He who looks upon the—'"

"Yes, I remember," said Traile. "Why?"

"It's already come true," Eric exclaimed. "You looked at the skull, and in a few minutes you killed a man. If you hadn't, you would have died."

"Only a coincidence," muttered Traile. But he glanced down at the thing beside him. The Golden Skull seemed to leer back mockingly at him.

CHAPTER 4
THE INVISIBLE EMPEROR

I N AN otherwise dark room hidden beneath Manhattan, one eye of a small Buddha suddenly glowed with emerald light. A yellow hand reached out from the gloom, and a sharp-nailed finger touched the rim of what appeared to be a roulette wheel. As the numbered wheel turned, the second eye of the Buddha became green, until it glowed with the same intensity as the first.

"Report," came the emotionless voice of the man seated beside the Buddha.

"Control, Group Three," a whisper came from the lips of the Buddha. "The police and Federal agents still hold position H. Number Ninety-three, using reporter's credentials, penetrated grounds and mansion. No prisoners observed, and no sign of—the Skull." The last two words were in an oddly altered tone.

A pointed saffron face, like a mocking picture of Satan, appeared for a moment above the wheel. In the emerald glow from the Buddha's eyes it was a weird hue.

"Police statements in regard to Citizen Fourteen?" the Yellow Doctor inquired.

"Removal believed underworld vengeance for refusing tribute to racketeers," was the muffled response from the Buddha. "This evidently based on report from Department of Justice agent in charge."

The tawny eyes slowly narrowed.

"Maintain close observation on the Federal officers. For some reason, they are withholding information. Courtland's son mentioned the Invisible Empire before he died."

THE EYES of the idol dimmed, then one went dark. Doctor Yen Sin leaned over the table on which the wheel and the Buddha stood. There was a row of pearl buttons in an onyx panel. He pressed the second button from the right. A faint, irregular buzzing sounded from the idol, and the numbered wheel began to rotate slowly.

The Crime Emperor sat back, a shadowy figure in the fan-backed Bilibid chair. A minute passed, and the wheel began its second revolution. Suddenly it stopped, swung back through an arc of forty degrees. Doctor Yen Sin reached out a yellow claw, and the buzzing signal ceased. Instantly the Buddha's eyes lit up.

"Group One," a sullen voice said.

The Yellow Doctor leaned forward.

"Your signal was transmitted at four fifty-three and five nineteen," he said coldly.

"I heard it, but couldn't answer," the other man said with a trace of harshness. "A bullet damaged the set, and I've just repaired it."

Yen Sin gazed down at the numbered wheel. It was still moving, but almost imperceptibly.

"You have had time to reach Headquarters B. Why are you still in motion?"

"It's taken all this time to shake off the police," came the muttered retort. "We're lucky we weren't killed."

The Crime Emperor looked unseeingly at the green eyes of the Buddha.

"Present orders revoked," he said with a return to his usual emotionless voice. "You will bring the Skull at once to Headquarters A."

There was a pause, then the Buddha rasped out the answer.

"We didn't get it! There was a mix-up—Agent Eighty-five had it—someone got it away from her in the dark."

A look of fury swept over the malignant face of Doctor Yen Sin. But when he spoke, his voice was icily controlled.

"Full report," he ordered.

"When we reached there," the voice from the idol said hoarsely, "Number Three entered, with Two and Five following. I heard a shot and ran after the others. I found Number Three slightly wounded, and Agent Eighty-five captured by a man who was evidently a police officer. This man shot and killed Number Two, then knocked over the candles. Agent Eighty-five was fleeing with the Skull when it was snatched from her hands. The place was almost surrounded—we barely had time to carry out Number Two and escape."

In the green light from the Buddha's eyes, the Crime Emperor's face held a furious look.

"Transfer to Agent Eighty-five," he directed.

"She escaped in the other car," was the sullen reply from the idol. "We separated at once."

There was a long interval, during which faint sounds of traffic came through from the microphone in the distant car.

"Follow these orders," Doctor Yen Sin said abruptly. He spoke for two minutes, then depressed a button. The Buddha's eyes dimmed, glowed again as the indicator wheel swung to its former position.

"Control, Group Three."

"Main Control," Yen Sin now said swiftly. "The Golden Skull was not recovered. Concentrate for necessary action. Groups Four and Five will reinforce you. Report at once any movement on part of the Federal men."

AS THE light faded from the idol's eyes, he stood up, the silken folds of his mandarin costume falling about his figure.

The arm of the skeleton quivered—then crumbled into rainbow-colored dust.

Though the room was now completely dark, he stretched out his hand to the exact spot where a light switch was located. A soft luminance spread over the room, revealing the details of the secret chamber. A richly colored Arabian rug, hung like a tapestry, covered most of one wall. Across from it was a large blackboard, on which were written words in both English and Chinese. In the center of the board was a sketch not unlike that of some intricate football maneuver.

On a rosewood table beside a divan was a tray bearing a teapot, a cup, and an empty dish, testimony to the sparse diet to which the Yellow Doctor adhered. Books and a number of photographs, the latter varying from miniatures to enlargements, cluttered one corner. A map case partly obscured a full-length mirror of peculiarly dark glass.

Doctor Yen Sin turned to an odd diagram which had been painted on one wall. It appeared to be a sketch showing the arrangement of streets in a small village. Colored lights showed at the ends of the streets and at some intersections. Beneath the diagram was a switchboard with a built-in Dictaphone.

The Crime Emperor inserted a plug in a socket, and one of the lights immediately flickered. He spoke in Chinese for a few moments, made another connection.

"Yes, Master?" came the hasty query, also in Chinese.

"What report from Group Six concerning the captives?" Doctor Yen Sin asked a trifle sharply.

"They have not appeared or reported, Master," the other man replied anxiously.

"Broaden the beam and search the area near Position D,"

ordered the Yellow Doctor. "There is a chance they have been forced into the other headquarters. Let me know the result."

"Yes, Master." The Dictaphone clicked. Doctor Yen Sin turned away. He crossed the room, moving with an almost feline step, and halted before the map case. He stood there a moment, his weird eyes flitting over the crayon lines which had been drawn on a chart of Long Island Sound. In the slant of his cheekbones, and by his height—for he was taller than most Chinese—an expert might have traced the Manchurian blood which coursed in the veins of the Yellow Doctor.

He glanced aside, stooped, and picked up one of the enlarged photographs. It was a gruesome scene—a tableau of murder. A crumpled body upon the floor... a dark stain on the man's shirtfront... the half-crouched form of the murderer, with a dripping knife in his hand, and his startled, ghastly face turned toward the camera....

Doctor Yen Sin's thin lips curled. There was something comical about that look of horror and dismay. The poor fool had thought himself so clever. He had never dreamed that he had been led every step of the way into committing that murder. But since then there had been time for him to learn.

A sudden clicking, as of distant castanets, caused the Crime Emperor to wheel quickly. A bright red light was shining above the painted diagram. Another light was blinking where two lines intersected. Doctor Yen Sin hastily crossed to the switchboard. As he plugged a connection, a rough voice became audible through the Dictaphone.

"Don't be a little fool! What's one Chink more or less?"

"Are you crazy?" a feminine voice gasped. "The Emperor will kill you for this."

"If he's so tough," came the grated answer, "why's he scared to show himself? I've still got to see the Chink I can't handle."

The girl moaned something, but the man cut her short.

"Get smart, baby! I've been watching you, and you got class enough for Ricco. We can take it on the lam before anybody gets wise. I can get a hundred grand for that rock, out on the Coast. You play along with Ricco, and you'll—"

"Let go of me!" the girl cried out.

Sounds of a scuffle came through the Dictaphone. Doctor Yen Sin calmly pressed a button, reached toward a switch at one side.

"You she-devil!" came a snarl from the unseen man. "I was goin' to give ya a break, but now—"

The sepulchral note of a deep-toned gong broke into his angry threat. In the same moment, light shone through the dark glass at one side of the secret room. The Yellow Doctor glanced toward the glass as footsteps echoed through the amplifier. A short passage was visible, its walls decorated with scores of red-and-gold circles. Each had a black center.

In a second, two figures came into view. The first was Iris Vaughan. Her blond hair was flying, and her pretty face was transfixed with a look of terror. Both greed and fear showed on the swarthy face of the man who pursued her. With a sudden leap, he caught the girl by one shoulder and spun her around. A brutal jerk, and he tore the jewel case from her fingers. A violent shove sent her back against the dark glass.

THE DEEP-TONED gong struck, and there followed a thudding sound from beyond the turn of the passage. The thief's swarthy face turned pasty. He whirled, the jewel case in one hand, a blood-smeared stiletto raised in the other. As he turned, the Yellow Doctor coolly threw a switch. The dark glass slid silently into a niche, and Iris Vaughan stumbled, almost fell into the room.

There was another thud, and a massive gate settled into place where the passage turned. As the gangster saw his escape cut off he sprang around with an oath. Then he froze.

From each of those red-and-gold circles a dark-stained blade was swiftly moving outward!

"You yellow butcher!" Ricco screamed. He hurled himself at the Crime Emperor. The stiletto flashed up—and scraped to a stop in midair. Behind the clear glass panel which had replaced the dark one, Doctor Yen Sin slowly smiled.

"You expressed a desire to see me, Mr. Ricco?" came his sibilant voice from some spot above the passage.

A tortured shriek burst from the gangster's lips as the swords began to gash his sides. He twisted around madly, pounding upon the glass.

"For God's sake, don't kill me! I didn't mean it—I'll do anything!"

The last word rose to a cry of mortal anguish. Iris Vaughan cowered away, hiding her face in her hands. The Yellow Doctor reached out toward the switchboard, and the faint whir of a hidden motor rose to a whine. One last dreadful scream rang out. Then Ricco's pierced body sagged, quivering, on the blades which had taken his life.

Without emotion, Doctor Yen Sin opened the heavy glass panel. He picked up the jewel case, calmly glanced at its contents. Stepping back into the secret room, he turned to the Dictaphone.

"The post of Number Five, Group Eight, is vacant," he announced tonelessly. "Correct the rolls and make the following disposal of the body." He spoke briefly in Chinese, then turned his tawny eyes on Iris Vaughan. The girl's face was sick with fear.

"I couldn't help it," she whispered. "He was hiding there at the third entrance. He sprang and killed Lun Shan—"

"The book of Mr. Ricco has been closed," said the Yellow Doctor. "But there is another matter—of real importance."

At the sudden harshness in his voice, the girl spoke breathlessly.

"I was hurrying to tell you. I reached the mansion ahead of—"

"The details have been reported," interrupted the Crime Emperor. "All but one." His weird eyes bored into her. "Who has the Golden Skull?"

"Michael Traile," she answered, and there was renewed dread in her face.

The pupils of Yen Sin's eyes enlarged with incredible swiftness, until they were black pools of fury. He took a step toward the girl, one yellow claw clenched.

"I did all I could!" she cried piteously. "But he tricked even the Gray Men."

There was a sharp buzzing, and the eyes of the Buddha glowed with green light. Doctor Yen Sin opened a sliding door which had been concealed by a tapestry.

"Be in readiness at your station," he curtly ordered. As the blond girl hurried out he closed the door and stooped over the idol. "Main Control. What report on Position H?"

"Federal men leaving in three cars," was the hasty reply. "Believe the Golden Skull in second car. Man observed carrying something under his coat. Did not observe personally but from description believe him to be Michael Traile. Senior Agent Allen and two men with machine guns in rear seat. Machine guns also in cars forming close escort. Success of direct action extremely doubtful."

Doctor Yen Sin looked down. The numbered wheel was moving very slowly.

"Maintain contact without arousing suspicion," he ordered. "Repeat this order to cooperating groups, then shift to Number Three waveband. Further instructions will follow."

As the wheel ceased to move, the Buddha's eyes changed to clear white light.

"Send Sonya to me at once," Yen Sin directed. "Then stand by for special code to Headquarters B."

Two minutes later a girl entered from the direction in which Iris Vaughan had disappeared. She was lovely, with a foreign, exotic beauty in which the warmth of sunny Spain and the cool aloofness of a Russian aristocrat were oddly blended. Her dark eyes, as she faced the Yellow Doctor, had a tragic, hopeless look. Yen Sin smiled mirthlessly at her.

"I have need of your talents, my dear Sonya." The tone was a deliberate mockery.

The girl's glance shifted to the gruesome figure suspended on the bloody swords in the passage. She stepped back in horror.

"No, it is neither of our expected—guests," said the Crime Emperor silkily. "They have been delayed, unfortunately." He had spoken in Chinese, but he abruptly changed to Russian. As he finished speaking, Sonya faced him with blazing eyes.

"No! I will not do it!" she cried defiantly. "This is some trick to make me help trap them again."

The oblique eyes of Doctor Yen Sin drew into slits.

"I have a photograph of your honorable father, taken as he received your last little—gift. Perhaps if I let you see it—"

All the fiery rebellion died out of her face.

"I'll go," she said in a broken voice. Her shoulders were drooping as she turned away. When she had gone, Doctor Yen Sin turned again to the Buddha. White light flashed, then swiftly he began his instructions.

CHAPTER 5
THE RAINBOW DEATH

TRAILE'S EYES searched the street ahead. "We're too well-guarded for him to try a mass attack," he said grimly. "If he strikes, it will be something unexpected."

"It's only three more blocks," said Eric. "Looks as though we'll get through O.K."

"I still think you've got this Yellow Doctor overrated," Bill

Allen grunted from the rear seat. "I'll admit he pulled a fast one out there at the Courtland place, but he can't buck the whole police system of New York City."

Trail swung the car into Lexington Avenue.

"You still don't understand the Invisible Empire. Yen Sin's spies keep him informed, and he gets around the police by trickery."

"Well, I'd like to see him get around these tommy guns," retorted the lanky D.J. man.

Traile looked down at the miniature radio set.

"Too bad we didn't get a good cross-bearing," he said to Eric. "We've lost our chance to locate that station."

Eric's face shadowed, and Traile knew he was thinking of Sonya Damitri.

The leading D.J. car slowed as they neared the building which housed the F.B.I. offices. The hour was not yet seven, and there were but few cars parked along the street. Traile pulled in close to the first machine, and the other D.J. car stopped behind him.

Early pedestrians stared as the agents jumped out with their guns poised. Traile thrust the golden skull under his coat and motioned for Eric to bring the radios. Allen and his men closed in as they went toward the building.

They were almost at the entrance when there came a crash of shots from back of them. Traile wheeled. A limousine was drawing up at the curb across the avenue. Fifty feet behind it, and darting in diagonally, was a taxicab. Guns were blazing from the rear of the cab, and Traile saw one of the limousine windows shatter.

Three or four D.J. men were racing toward the spot. Two more shots crashed from the taxi, then a pinched yellow face glared around toward the running agents. A look of terror crossed the features of the Chinese. He frantically swerved his pistol.

Two tommy guns roared simultaneously. The Chinese toppled back, riddled with lead. The bloody face of a second Oriental was visible as the taxi wildly leaped ahead. As he slumped from view, another machine gun burst drilled both tires on the left side. The taxi skidded crazily, plunged headlong against a lamp-post and overturned. The driver fell out limply, lay still.

As the firing began, Traile shot a hurried look around the entrance and into the lobby. This might be an attempt by Yen Sin to draw attention so that other spies of the Invisible Empire could regain the skull. But there was no sign of an attack.

A crowd was beginning to gather in the street. A big man, of powerful build, had jumped from the rear of the limousine. As two of Allen's men approached, Traile saw the big man motion anxiously, then all three bent over the crumpled form of the limousine chauffeur.

"Jumping Jupiter!" Allen erupted. "That's Mark Bannister those Chink gunmen tried to rub out!"

"Another millionaire," Traile muttered, half to himself. "I wonder what Yen Sin is after."

IN A moment Bannister hurried toward them with one of the agents. Traile would hardly have recognized the financier, though he had seen pictures of him. In addition to being a financial power, with his hotels, his steamship line, and his brokerage house, Mark Bannister was known as a Beau Brummel. But now his handsome face was haggard with fear and strain. His cheeks were unshaven, and there were dark circles under his eyes. Blood was dripping from a small cut on his jaw, where flying glass had struck.

"Which one?" he rasped to the man beside him, as he reached the group.

"This is Special Agent Allen," said the other, indicating the lanky D.J. man.

The millionaire jerked around to Allen.

"I'm Mark Bannister. I want to see you—alone!"

Allen hesitated, glanced at Traile. Traile spoke in an undertone.

"You question him first, while I examine the skull up in your lab."

Allen motioned to one of his men.

"Take charge, Weller. Find out all you can, and explain to the cops what happened."

Traile and Eric entered an elevator with the millionaire and Bill Allen. The operator looked, wide-eyed, from Allen's tommy gun to the cut on Bannister's jaw. The financier glared at him, stamped out at the fourteenth floor, almost failing over a wrinkled old charwoman who was mopping up the corridor.

As Bannister and Allen disappeared into an office, Traile nodded for Eric to follow him into the laboratory. The technician on duty was a pleasant-faced agent named Jim Stone. Traile knew him from a former visit, when Director Glover had introduced him as Roger Scott, a private criminologist who was to be given the run of the place.

"What happened down below?" Stone asked, after Traile introduced Eric. "I heard the shooting, but couldn't see much from the window."

Traile explained briefly.

"Hell's bells!" said Stone. "That and the Courtland murder will split the town wide open."

"How did you know about Courtland?" Traile asked sharply. "Police teletype?"

"No, there was a radio news flash almost an hour ago. All about his head being sewed on backward and—" Stone stared as Traile brought the gold skull from under his coat. "What the devil is the idea of that?"

"That's what we want to know," said Traile as he put the skull down on a table. "Let me have a magnifying glass, will you? I haven't had time for a careful examination."

"You mean you found this thing?" exclaimed Stone, amazed.

Traile hesitated only a moment.

"It was at the head of Courtland's coffin, but don't mention that to anyone. I'm explaining to you because there's some danger connected with it, and it will have to be closely guarded."

Professional interest quickly conquered Stone's first astonishment. He brought a magnifying glass, switched on a bright light. Traile took the glass, bent over the gleaming skull, and looked through the eye sockets. After a brief scrutiny he carefully turned it upside down and peered in through the throat opening. The skull was empty, and except for a few scratches the interior of the metal shell was unmarked.

"What did you expect to find?" asked Eric, as Traile straightened up with a look of disappointment.

"I thought some secret of the cult might be engraved inside," Traile answered a trifle shortly. The puzzle was beginning to annoy him.

"Maybe it's written so small that this glass won't show it up," suggested Stone. "I can put it under the big microscope."

"I don't think there's anything to see," said Traile. "But you might as well try it."

STONE STARTED to pick up the skull, then grasped it in both hands. "Say, that thing's heavy! I wouldn't mind having what it's worth in cash."

"It's probably worth about ten thousand dollars," stated Traile. "But I've had proof that it's valued for some other reason."

"Ten thousand bucks would be plenty of reason for me," said Eric.

"Same here," grinned Stone. He carried the skull over to a large compound microscope and was placing it on the stage when Allen hastily entered the room. Behind the agent came Bannister. Allen closed the door, turned to Traile and addressed him by the name he had temporarily assumed.

"Scott, I've already told Mr. Bannister that you're working with us on this Courtland case. He has some information that should help us.

"It's help for myself I want," the millionaire said bluntly. His hard eyes probed at Traile. "You saw what happened down there—I escaped death by a miracle—my bodyguard was murdered—"

"Bodyguard?" said Traile.

"He was acting as chauffeur," snapped Bannister, "because the regular man disappeared—vanished like five more of my employees! I tell you it's maddening—knowing there's something closing in on you—knowing there are eyes watching you all the time."

He looked around fiercely at Eric and Stone, who were both staring at him, then pulled a crumpled paper from his coat pocket.

"Here's a sample of what I mean. Read that, and for 'Citizen Nine' substitute 'Mark Bannister!'"

The message was typewritten in green ink. Traile's dark eyes passed quickly over the words.

SECRET REPORT 31 ON CITIZEN NINE
DATE: JULY 17, 8 P.M. TO MIDNIGHT

At 8:03, Citizen 9 called from his penthouse apartment on top Hotel Lordmore, speaking by direct wire to the hotel manager. Gave instructions that Citizens 12 and 14 were to be brought up secretly from garage in basement—

"Think of it!" rasped Bannister. "One of my own hotels—my private wire! But go on—go on!"

Citizens 12 and 14 arrived by private penthouse elevator at 8:10. During dinner, Citizen 14 produced copy of latest secret report on his movements. Announced he was going to the police. Citizens 9 and 12 argued against this, but at 10:35 he left for that purpose. At 11:15, Citizen 12 departed after phoning down to his private detective escort to meet him on mezzanine floor. Citizen 9 stationed special guard at switchboard controlling the private elevator, with orders to keep current shut off. Retired at 11:50, after searching entire apartment.

Traile looked up slowly.

"Is this report accurate?"

"It's exact!" the millionaire said harshly. "The thing is uncanny. Our conference didn't start until dinner had been served and my servants had been sent downstairs."

Traile studied the lower edge of the paper.

"A piece had been cut off here. Did you do it?"

Bannister did not answer for a moment. Then he rammed his hands into his coat pockets and spoke abruptly.

"All right, I'll tell you! I've received thirty of those damned reports, some even describing things I thought nobody could possibly know. Each one has contained mention of something private, personal." He made a savage gesture. "Every man in my position has made mistakes on the way up. But how these devils ever learned—"

"Then it's blackmail?" Traile asked calmly.

"It must be!" grated Bannister. "But they haven't asked a cent. After each report—except this one—I've had a mysterious phone call. I've been told to go to a certain place to meet someone—but a different spot has been named every time. I've gone three times, with private detectives hiding nearby—but no one appeared."

"If you'd come to us sooner—" began Allen, but the millionaire cut him off with a snort.

"Never mind about that! I'm here now and I want protection. I heard the news that Courtland's been murdered, and after what just occurred I know I must be next on the list."

Traile looked at him keenly.

"The man called 'Citizen Fourteen' in this message was Peter Courtland, wasn't he?"

Bannister started.

"What makes you think that?"

"It's evident that no rich man complained to the police about being threatened," said Traile, "or the detectives on the Courtland case would have seen a connection. It's fair to assume that he was seized on his way to Centre Street."

THE HAGGARD expression came back into the millionaire's face. "You're right, it was old Courtland. He and Merton Cloyd came last night to help me form a scheme to fight this mysterious group. They were getting reports like this, too."

Allen cleared his throat.

"You and the others hadn't any idea, then, who was back of the letters?"

Bannister started to shake his head, then paused.

"Cloyd and I didn't, but something last night made me think that Courtland knew more than he was telling. I asked him if he'd made contact with these devils. He denied it, but the way he acted—"

A woman's querulous voice was suddenly audible from out in the hall. Its shrill accents were cut off by a muttered snarl and the sound of a blow. As Allen ran to the side door there was a stifled cry, and a clatter of something against the panels.

"Be careful!" rapped Traile. "Stand to one side when you open it!"

Allen gripped the knob, jumped back. As the door opened, the handle of a mop slid down and struck the floor. Just beyond, the old charwoman was struggling to her feet, a bruise on her wrinkled face. Traile helped her up.

"Thanks, sir—but I'll be all right now," she said in a quavering voice.

"What happened?" Allen demanded.

The old woman whimpered, rubbing her bruised cheek.

"It was a man, sir—I come on him sudden-like, and there he was, with his ear to the door, listenin'—"

"What did he look like? Which way did he go?" Allen broke in impatiently.

"His face was queer—almost like a dead man's." The old woman looked fearfully toward the stairs to the lower floors. "You'd best be careful—he's a bad one."

"It must have been one of the Gray Men," Traile said to Allen in a lowered voice. "If you work fast, you may be able to catch him."

Allen dashed toward the front offices, and in a few moments his agents were spreading out in a hasty search. The old charwoman picked up her mop and bucket, shuffled down the hall. Traile turned back into the laboratory as he saw that Stone had come into the hall with Bannister and Eric.

"We shouldn't have left the skull unguarded," he said anxiously.

"Nobody could've come through from the front," replied the technician. "There are always three or four men up there."

Traile locked the door as Bannister and Eric followed him into the room. Stone switched on one of the special illuminators attached to the microscope.

The millionaire gave a puzzled look at the skull, then glanced back at Traile.

"You appear to have influence here. I want some of your agents to guard me."

"My connection is unofficial," said Traile. "But Allen can probably arrange it."

As he started out with Bannister, he turned to Eric.

"You'd better stay here with Stone. Keep your gun ready, in case you hear anyone else at that door."

When they reached Allen's office, the senior agent was just putting down the phone.

"No luck yet," be said irritably, "but I'm having all entrances watched."

The millionaire gruffly stated his request for D.J. agents to guard him. Allen hesitated.

"So far, Mr. Bannister, it's not a Federal case. The Courtland murder and the attack on you are police matters. Those secret reports don't actually constitute a crime."

"What about the abduction of my servants—my two secretaries?" rasped Bannister. "I came here because I don't want publicity. The police will spread it all over the papers. You people have a reputation for doing things quietly."

Allen gave Traile a sidewise glance. "What do you think?"

Traile's dark eyes rested on the millionaire's haggard face.

"Mr. Bannister, have you ever heard of the Invisible Empire?"

Bannister shook his head.

"No, what is it?"

"It's the organization back of those reports," replied Traile.

AN ANGRY color darkened Bannister's face. "If you already know about this business, why didn't you say so?"

"I didn't know about the letters," Traile said calmly. "But from the Courtland evidence—"

He stopped as Eric Gordon burst into the office.

"Come on!" Eric exclaimed. There was an excited light in his blue eyes. "Stone's found out something."

All three men jumped to their feet.

"What is it?" clipped Traile, as they hurried toward the laboratory.

"I don't know," Eric said tensely. "He said one of the light rays showed up some writing that seemed to be inside the metal. Then all of a sudden he got a scared look, and sent me back here to get you."

"It may be the key to the whole thing," Allen said in an eager voice.

Traile nodded, started through the room adjoining the laboratory. He was halfway to the connecting door when a muffled hissing became audible from the other room. Then a voice rose in a scream of agony.

"It's Stone!" shouted Allen.

Traile sprang for the door. He flung it open, then jumped back in amazement. A cloud of weirdly beautiful smoke was swirling within the laboratory. In its opaque, shimmering haze shone every hue of the rainbow.

Somewhere from the depths of that pastel-colored smoke came a terrible, frenzied cry. It died away, and there was only the muffled hissing which had been heard at first.

The opening of the door had brought some of the smoke billowing into the other room. It puffed into Traile's face, stinging his eyes. He stumbled against Bannister. Then, realizing that the smoke was not immediately poisonous, he drew a deep breath of fresh air and dashed into the laboratory.

Through the eddying smoke he glimpsed something jerking around madly near the center of the room. He could vaguely see flashes of colored light, like fireworks seen through a heavy fog. The hissing came from that spot.

Half-blinded, he managed to find a window and raise it. Not until the colored smoke had blown away from where he stood did he risk taking a breath. The rest of the room was still hidden from view. He could hear Allen coughing, and the others stumbling around in the smoke.

"Keep back until it's clear!" he called out.

A figure staggered toward him, almost collapsed at the open window. It was Bannister.

"What is it?" gasped the millionaire.

"I don't know," Traile answered tautly. He strained his eyes for a sign of Jim Stone. The hissing began to diminish, and in a few moments it had ended. The eerie smoke dissipated rapidly as fresh air blew into the room.

As Allen and Eric Gordon appeared in the colored haze, Traile stepped toward the center of the laboratory. The queer flashes of light had ceased with the hissing, but the last of that strange and beautiful smoke still hovered over the spot.

As it started to fade, a bony hand became visible. Then swiftly the smoke thinned, revealing the dreadful thing which lay beneath. Traile stared down in stark horror.

There on the floor was a rainbow-colored skeleton! It was all that remained of Jim Stone.

CHAPTER 6
THE WOMAN IN RAGS

A LLEN SWAYED back, white and sick. "Oh, my God!" he whispered.

Eric and Bannister looked down with stunned faces at the shimmering, gruesome figure. Faint wisps of colored smoke still eddied around the rainbow-hued skeleton. The effect was one of horrible beauty, more dreadful than bleached white bones would have been.

"Oh, God!" Allen said again. He pulled his eyes away, looked dazedly at Traile. "What terrible thing—"

Traile shook his head, then knelt down, his lean face pale under its tan. A slight breeze was blowing in from the opened window. Suddenly the left arm of the skeleton quivered, then a tiny cloud of bright ashes fluttered into the air. The next moment the hand and forearm crumbled into rainbow-colored dust.

Traile stood up and quickly closed the window. But the crumbling process continued, until in a minute, only a vague-shaped, sinister pile of colored ash remained on the marble floor. He gazed at it a moment longer, then with a start turned to the big microscope. In the horror of his discovery, he had forgotten the golden skull. Allen followed his swift glance.

"It's gone!" he said hoarsely.

Traile bent over the mounting stage to which the skull had been fastened. One side was mottled with the same colors as those of the rainbow ashes. He heard an exclamation, looked up into Allen's tortured face.

"The stuff that killed him must have been a part of the skull!" rasped the D.J. man.

"No," Traile said grimly, "he was killed by something else, so that someone could get the skull out of here. Look at this clamp. It's twisted from a jerk, and there's a scraping of gold on the setscrew."

Eric Gordon ran across to the hall door.

"It's still locked," he exclaimed.

"A master key would take care of that," rapped Traile. He wheeled to the half-dazed Allen. "They'll be trying to get it out of the building. It's doubly important now—"

A savage look replaced the sickness in the senior agent's eyes.

"By God, if I catch the fiend who did this—" the rest was lost as he ran toward the front offices.

His whirlwind exit sent a flurry of rainbow ash into the air. Bannister stared at it and shivered. Traile turned to Eric.

"Did Stone give you any other hint of what he learned about the skull?"

"Not a word," mumbled Eric. "But whatever he saw, it gave him a bad scare. He jumped back and told me to get you as fast as I could. I may be wrong, but I think it was something beside the writing that scared him."

"I should have had a dozen men in here guarding him," Traile said self-accusingly. "I might have known something would happen."

"Why was that little gold skull so important?" Bannister interposed curiously.

Traile's bronzed face was stern. "Because Courtland's murderers left it at the head of his coffin."

The millionaire started.

"But why, in Heaven's name?" Traile was hurrying from window to window, examining the ledges.

"I believe it was a mistake," he answered. "Since then, agents of the Invisible Empire have tried desperately to recover it. And now they've succeeded, unless—" He stopped short.

"What's the matter?" Eric asked. "The charwoman!" Traile whirled toward the door to the hall. "I was a fool not to guess it before."

HE JERKED open the door, then spun around to Bannister. "Warn Allen not to let that woman get out of the building! We'll be searching for her at once." Eric raced after him to the rear elevator shafts. When a car came up, Traile shot a sharp look at the attendant and then spoke. "Have you seen the charwoman who works on this floor?"

"Ya mean the new one?" said the operator. "She's up on Sixteen. I saw her a few minutes ago."

Traile sprang into the car.

"Take us up!" When they reached the floor, he flung a crisp order at the man. "Go back to Fourteen and find Mr. Allen— Bureau of Investigation. Tell him to rush a squad up here!"

"Yes, sir!" gulped the operator. The car started down. Traile drew a fresh cartridge clip from a leather pocket under his belt.

"Take the left corridor," he whispered to Eric, as he rammed the magazine into his gun. "She'll probably have other spies helping her, so be on your guard."

A determined look came into Eric's youthful face. He hurried away on tiptoe. Traile took the other hall, watching each door that he passed. It was only seven thirty, and all the offices still appeared to be deserted. He made a right-angle turn, was almost to the next one when he saw an open window at the end of a side corridor leading to a fire escape. As he started toward it, Eric appeared from the other direction.

"No sign of her—" the younger man began.

"Quiet," whispered Traile. He leaned out warily, then straightened. "There's a window open in the second office to the left. Cover the door while I sneak in from this direction."

He stole out onto the fire escape, noiselessly made his way to the office window. As he reached it he heard a gasp, then he saw the charwoman run for the door. She threw it open, then gave a moan as Eric confronted her in the shadowy entrance.

Traile saw her cringe away from him, a wretched figure in tattered black, her streaked gray hair tumbling down over her eyes.

"Watch her, Eric!" he said sharply. "She's a cold-blooded murderess!"

Eric made no answer. Traile climbed through the window, after a quick glance to be sure that no one else was in the room. As he saw the torment in Eric's eyes, he grasped their captive's shoulder and pulled her around. A strange sight met his gaze.

Gone were the wrinkled features of the old charwoman. Only a smudge of make-up here and there remained to betray the secret. An oval face, lovely with a foreign, exotic charm, looked up at him in despair.

"Good God!" he said, half under his breath. He reached out toward the tangled hair. Two slim hands, no longer gnarled, flew up to her head, but it was too late. As he lifted away the wig, the lustrous black hair of a beautiful woman was revealed. The last faint hope vanished from Eric Gordon's blue eyes.

"Sonya!" he groaned. "To think you could do that awful thing!"

A haunted look crossed her face.

"I didn't kill him," she said in a shaken voice. "It was only intended to drive him from the room while—"

"While you stole the golden skull," Traile finished grimly. "But you killed him, nevertheless."

"No, no! I was not the—" she broke off, drew herself up with a quiet dignity. "Arrest me if you will. I am a criminal—yes. But I have never killed anyone."

ERIC HAD come into the room, was watching her in misery. But at her last words some of the hope came back into his face.

"Michael, she's telling the truth! Look at her eyes—you can see—"

Traile smiled bitterly.

"I'm afraid your infatuation has blinded you, Eric."

"It's not infatuation!" Eric burst out hotly. "If she weren't any good, I'd never care—"

A slow flush came into Sonya Damitri's pale cheeks as he left the sentence unfinished.

Traile broke in coldly before she could speak.

"Even if you're telling the truth, you're still an accessory to murder."

"Didn't you hear?" Eric cried fiercely. "She wasn't the one who did it—she's innocent!"

The girl gave him a sad smile from under her long black lashes.

"I shall never forget—that you believed in me," she said softly.

There was a sudden movement in the doorway.

"Good work?" came a muffled snarl "Raise your hands—you two!"

Traile had wheeled as the man appeared. There in the doorway stood one of the gray-faced men. His oddly sunken eyes glared over a leveled gun. For a split second, Traile hesitated, but Eric was in his line of fire Slowly, he raised his hands. The Gray Man stepped into the room. He closed the door, snatched Eric's gun and thrust it into his pocket.

"Get the other one," he harshly ordered Sonya. His bloodless lips seemed hardly to move when he spoke.

The girl hastily took Traile's gun, laid it on a desk. He saw her wince before the look in Eric's eyes.

"Where is the Golden Skull?" demanded the Gray Man. His queer eyes flicked toward the dirty water in the bucket which Sonya had carried.

"It's still in there," she said in a low voice. "They haven't dropped the line."

"It will be down in a few seconds," said the man. "Be ready to hook on the bucket while I take care of these two."

A frightened light came into her great black eyes.

"You can't kill them!" Her expression quickly altered, under his penetrating glare. "The last orders were that they were to be taken alive."

"There's no chance for that now," retorted the Gray Man. "I'd better finish them."

"You know the penalty for disobeying!" the girl exclaimed. "Tie them up, or lock them in that closet."

Something scraped, out on the fire escape. Sonya picked up the bucket and carried it to the window. As the Gray Man drove the two captives toward the closet, Traile saw a hook dangling just outside. The girl grasped it, and in a moment he saw the bucket disappear upward.

"Hurry up and finish changing," the Gray Man muttered nervously. "Those agents may be up here any minute."

Sonya took up a thick briefcase from the desk, and ran into

67

the room adjoining the office. The man twitched his gun toward Eric.

"Reach back and open that door. And don't try any tricks."

Eric obeyed in angry silence. The Gray Man cast a hasty look into the closet, evidently searching for something to bind and gag the two men. Traile had not moved, after being forced back toward the wall, but his dark eyes never left their captor's face. Suddenly the Gray Man stiffened.

"Turn around!" he said in a muffled tone.

Eric started to obey, but Traile halted him with a swift warning.

"Watch out! He intends to slug you!"

The Gray Man lunged toward him, stopped with a snarled oath, swerving his gun back and forth to cover them.

"Turn around, both of you!" he rasped. "Unless you want a dose of lead!"

Eric tensed, but Traile signaled with a jerk of his head.

"Hold it! He doesn't dare kill us."

THERE WAS a gasp, and Sonya reappeared. The ragged dress of the charwoman had been replaced by a smart knitted suit, and a small sport hat covered her dark hair. Instead of the shabby shoes, she wore a pair of modish pumps. "What are you doing?" she demanded. "I told you—*look out!*"

Her cry was directed at Eric. In the brief instant when the Gray Man's gaze jerked toward her, Eric had crouched for a spring. But the other man had whirled, lifting his gun for a furious blow. Traile hurtled between him and Eric. The butt of the pistol, descending with a force that would have crushed Eric's skull, struck Traile's shoulder.

That sudden leap had knocked Eric backward into the closet. The impact of the gun numbed Traile's left arm, swung him around. He lashed out with his right, and the Gray Man's pistol jetted flame toward the ceiling. But before Traile could wrest the gun from his hand, a vicious blow to the stomach sent him reeling. The door slammed as he fell against Eric, then the lock clicked, and the voices of Sonya and the Gray Man quickly died away.

It was half a minute before Traile could get his breath from that blow to his solar plexus. Eric frantically bent over him in the dark.

"Michael! Oh, good Lord, he's been shot!"

"No—only took my wind," Traile managed to groan. He pulled himself to his feet. "We've got to break out of here."

He turned his uninjured shoulder, and together they crashed against the door. At the second attempt, a panel splintered. As the door burst open, Allen and three of his men charged into the room.

"What the hell?" yelped the senior agent as he recognized them.

"No time to explain!" said Traile. "They hauled the skull up to the roof!"

"They must be crossing to the next building," snapped Allen. He and his agents raced for the elevators.

Traile's gun was still lying on the desk. He picked it up, went out into the hall. Another squad of agents appeared. Traile tersely described Sonya while Eric stood by unhappily. The operatives quickly separated to look for her and continue their search for the Gray Man. Traile and Eric silently went down to the fourteenth floor.

Ten minutes later a glum-faced group assembled in Allen's office.

"They're a slick outfit, all right," growled the senior agent. "They got away clean."

"What about the girl?" Eric asked, staring at the floor.

The agent named Weller spoke up.

"She went right out the front way, before we got the second warning." He grinned ruefully. "When you're looking for an old charwoman, you don't stop a classy dame like that."

Traile was the only one who saw the relief in Eric's eyes. There was a brief silence, then he turned to Bannister.

"Do you happen to know whether Harley Kent still owns the Vare Diamond?"

The millionaire looked surprised.

"So far as I know. Why?"

"I want to pay him a visit." Traile looked at Allen. "I think you'd better come, too."

"What about the protection I asked for?" said Bannister. In the last half-hour, his unshaven face had become more haggard than ever.

"You can go along with us," said Allen. "We'll talk over the details on the way."

As they went out, two men came along the hall which led to the laboratory. They were carefully carrying a porcelain tray with a pane of glass for a cover. As Traile glanced down, the hall lights sparkled in the rainbow dust which had once been a man.

CHAPTER 7
"YOU HAVE TILL
MIDNIGHT TO LIVE"

FOR ALMOST half an hour, the talking Buddha had been silent. Before the idol, the Yellow Doctor sat like some grim statue of Satan. His glittering, tawny eyes were fixed in space. Only the restless tapping of his talon-like fingers betrayed the tension within him.

Suddenly the eyes of the Buddha glowed bright green. The Crime Emperor swiftly leaned forward.

"Main Control!" The words all but crackled.

"The Golden Skull is recovered," a voice said rapidly. "A Federal technician examining it was destroyed. Operating group safely withdrawn, and Agent Twenty-two also clear. No clues left unless by the Gray Man cooperating."

Dr. Yen Sin slowly sat back in his chair.

"What report on Michael Traile?"

"Left the building ten minutes ago with man known as Citizen Nine, Gordon, and Agent Allen," was the reply from the idol. "Gordon carried small black box strapped to what appeared to be a toy church. Party was delayed at the door by arrival of Police Commissioner, presumably investigating Courtland case, also by detectives covering the action in Lexington

71

Avenue. Traile and Allen conferred privately with the commissioner, then followed Gordon and Citizen Nine into a car. Personal observation transferred to Group Two."

The Crime Emperor touched one of the buttons before him. A buzzing was audible, and the numbered wheel began to rotate slowly. In a few seconds the Buddha's eyes, which had dimmed, shone brightly again.

"Group Two." A husky voice spoke against a muffled background of traffic sounds. "On Fifth Avenue, following car containing—"

"I am already informed," Dr. Yen Sin interrupted, "as to the occupants. Notify me at once when they arrive at Hotel Lordmore."

"They're not going to the Lordmore," came the hurried reply from the talking Buddha. "Observer in crowd overheard senior agent's orders to the escort, to follow them to residence of Harley Kent."

The Yellow Doctor's robed figure stiffened.

"This should have been reported at once!"

"We tried, but the signal wasn't answered," began the other nervously. "I thought—"

"Break contact!" said Dr. Yen Sin. "Proceed as rapidly as possible to the Kent residence. Assign one man to carry out these instructions." He spoke incisively for almost a minute. "Act at once on his signal. I shall delay the escorting agents, but count on no more than two minutes."

As the eyes of the idol darkened, the Crime Emperor quickly bent over the row of buttons before him.

WITH ERIC GORDON at the wheel, the sedan swung away from the curb, moving slowly through the crowd which had gathered. Michael Traile, seated in the rear with Bannister, glanced back carelessly. The car with the escorting agents was following at a short distance.

"I hope you don't expect another attack," Bannister said uneasily.

Traile shook his head.

"It's not likely, now. Beside, this car is armored and the windows are bulletproof."

The millionaire drew a breath of relief.

"Thank Heaven for that! I've had enough to last me for a long time."

"It beats me," Allan grated from the front seat, "how they've got away with everything. The Courtland affair was bad enough—but that damned business right in a Federal building—"

"I told you we were fighting a master criminal," Traile said a trifle wearily. He lighted a cigarette, leaned back and relaxed his tightened muscles. "Every important move he makes is planned like a military maneuver, with detailed orders to every man—or woman—involved."

From his position at the right, he could see Eric flush. Bannister shook his head.

"It's incredible, a thing like that here in Manhattan. If I hadn't had proof through those secret reports—"

"I was going to ask you about those," said Traile. His words had an oddly lazy note, the result of his complete relaxation. "Have you tried to trace the sender?"

"Yes, but it was useless," growled the millionaire. "Some came by ordinary mail, some by messengers who could give only vague descriptions of the person who paid for them. They've been sent to my Wall Street office, my hotels—even to my yacht."

Traile's dark eyes were on the rear-vision mirror up forward.

"The one this morning?" he asked absently.

Bannister scowled.

"It was at the desk when I hurried down. One of the clerks had heard the radio flash about poor old Courtland, and knowing our association he called me at once. When I reached the desk, he told me the letter had been brought in by a special messenger, about an hour before. It was marked *Urgent.*"

Traile gazed through the smoke from his cigarette.

"If we only knew his exact motive," he mused. "Blackmail, yes—but if I know the Invisible Emperor that's only a means to an end."

A queer hunted expression came into Bannister's eyes.

"Until this morning," he began slowly, "I never considered anything but plain blackmail. But after Courtland's murder—and those Chinese gunmen—" He hesitated, made an impatient gesture. "It's ridiculous, I suppose, but I suddenly recalled an episode which occurred in China almost six years ago."

Both Allen and Eric started, and Traile's bronzed face lost its indolent look.

"I didn't know you'd been in China," he said quickly.

74

The millionaire nodded.

"It was in connection with my importing business—my freight steamship line. I was there about a year, and I'd put over some pretty shrewd deals, when strange things began to happen. One of my ships caught fire—two of my confidential men disappeared—I was threatened with death unless I paid tribute to some mysterious Chinese. I fought back, but things became so bad that I had to leave. The officials at Shanghai told me that they were helpless—that this devil called the *Shek* would revenge himself if I ever returned."

"You're lucky to be alive," Traile said in a grim voice. "The man they called the 'Cobra' was none other than Doctor Yen Sin, the man we are seeking."

BANNISTER LOOKED at him in consternation. "What! You mean to say this Invisible Emperor is a Chinese?"

"Right—and in my opinion the most dangerous man alive! A super-scientist, an evil genius with the ruthless will of a dictator—and an Oriental hatred for the white race that amounts to a mania."

There was perspiration on the millionaire's forehead, and Traile saw the fear in his eyes.

"Then I was right," Bannister said hoarsely. "It's personal vengeance he's after."

Traile's eyes were again on the rear-vision mirror.

"Perhaps so," he muttered. "But in these other cases—" He whirled, stared through the window behind him.

"What's the matter?" exclaimed Allen.

"A suspicious-looking car has been following along with the

traffic," Traile answered. "I noticed it at one side of the escort machine when we left Lexington Avenue. It just now turned and dashed into Forty-fifth Street."

"You mean that black delivery truck?" cut in Eric.

"That's the one," said Traile. "But I've a hunch that it was no ordinary truck. There was no name on it. The driver and the man with him looked foreign. Also, that black glass in the side looked like the old speakeasy-door kind, the type you can see through and not be seen. There may have been more men inside."

As he spoke, Traile leaned down and switched on the miniature radio set.

"What's the idea of that?" queried Bannister.

Traile lifted the set to his knee.

"Doctor Yen Sin is using a special microwave radio to transmit orders to his agents. We caught one message, but—" He bent over quickly as one hand in the church-steeple quivered. "We're in the beam! He must be sending a message to those men in the truck."

"Then why don't we hear it?" objected Allen.

"They've shifted to a waveband out of our range, but the indicator is wired higher and it registers." Traile stared down at the trembling needle. "Step on it, Eric! Get to Kent's place as fast as you can!"

The sedan shot forward, grazed a bus, wove swiftly through traffic. At Forty-seventh Street, a policeman whistled peremptorily for them to slow down. Allen had already jerked his gold F.B.I. shield from an inner pocket. He flashed it, shouted at the officer. The sedan sped on. Two minutes later, as Eric was swinging left in the upper Fifties, Allen gave a startled exclamation.

"Wait a minute! We've lost the other car."

"We can't stop now," said Traile. "That may be part of the scheme, to cut them off."

"What do you think they're up to?" Bannister asked in alarm.

"It must be connected with the Vare Diamond," Traile responded crisply.

It was only half a block from Fifth Avenue to the old brownstone house which served as bachelor quarters for Harley Kent, well-known collector of rare jewels. As the sedan slid to a halt in front of the building, Traile looked quickly down the street. Then, still holding the micro-set, he jumped out and motioned for the others to follow.

"There's a chance they may have—" he stopped, as the door opened and a frightened-looking manservant came running down the steps.

"What's wrong?" Allen demanded.

"Mr. Kent—he's been murdered!" cried the man.

"Good Lord," rasped the F.B.I. agent. He sprang up the steps. Traile and the others quickly followed with the servant. As they entered, Traile shoved the strapped set under his arm and drew his .38.

"When did it happen?" he asked the manservant in a low tone.

"I don't know, sir," the man wailed. "I just came in and found him there—" he pointed a trembling hand into the library.

TRAILE PUSHED him ahead, cast a keen glance around

the hall before following Bannister and Eric into the room. Allen stood transfixed, a few feet from the doorway. Traile looked, then he, too, stopped in his tracks.

In a high-backed chair at the head of the library table sat Harley Kent. His hands were tied behind the chair, keeping his body from falling forward. A wide strip of purplish tape covered his lips, except at one spot where dark blood had oozed out and was slowly dropping. The dead man's eyes were open with an agonized stare.

But that tortured face, terrible as it was, held Traile's eyes only a moment. For Harley Kent had been stripped to the waist, and his bared chest stabbed three times with a red-hot iron. The three ugly wounds formed a triangle, with one hole over the heart, and directly in the center of the triangle was a tiny gilt seal. It was in the shape of a skull.

For a moment no one moved. Then Traile stepped close to the dead man.

"Another murder in the name of the *Chuen Gin Lou*," he said in a hard voice.

Eric looked down at the seal, and a grimace twitched his lips.

"Michael, that thing has the same hideous expression as the Golden Skull!"

Traile slowly nodded, stooped to look at the mutilating wounds in Harley Kent's breast. As he straightened, he saw the manservant shudder and turn away. Mark Bannister was gazing with a horrified fascination at the corpse.

"God!" he said thickly. "He must have gone through hell before he died."

Allen had not spoken since he entered. But as the servant stepped back, the lanky F.B.I. man suddenly bent over. He stood up with a large plush jewel case in his hands.

"This must be the answer," he said harshly. "The devils probably got away with some valuable stones."

Just as he started to open it, Traile caught a furtive movement near the door.

"Wait!" he rapped out. But it was too late. Even as he spoke, Allen pressed the catch. The lid of the jewel case flew open, and a dark, fragrant vapor instantly poured forth.

"The incense!" Eric cried thickly. He took a blind step forward, fell to his knees. Traile had sprung toward the doorway, where the servant was stealing out. But as the fragrant anesthetic engulfed him, an unwanted weakness sent him staggering. Allen and Bannister were both crumpling to the floor. A terrific pain shot through his head. He caught at the table, then as he saw the servant's tense face in the entry he let himself fall with a groan. The next second he heard the man racing up the hall toward the front of the house.

He pulled himself up, stumbled toward the door. While his sleepless brain refused to yield to the drug, a feeling of exhaustion threatened to overcome him. He forced himself on, gripped the knob and pulled the door open. The fresh air from the hall was like a dash of cold water in his face. He gulped in a deep breath, tightened his grasp on the pistol, which had almost slipped from his fingers.

From the entrance of the house came a peculiar whistle. Traile lunged toward the vestibule, sucking deep breaths into his lungs. As he reached the door, he saw the false servant signal hastily toward the street, then a motor roared, and the black truck swiftly drew up in front.

ABRUPTLY, THE other man turned and saw Traile. His pinched face contorted in amazement and terror. Then, like a cornered rat, he sprang. Traile's gun was already lifted. He slashed it fiercely along the side of the spy's head. With a howl, the man teetered backward, rolled down the steps.

Two men had leaped from the front seat of the truck. Dismay spread over their features as Traile appeared. One of them jumped back, shouting toward the rear of the machine. Instantly, a section of dark glass slid open in the side of the truck. The muzzled snout of a silenced machine gun poked up at Traile.

Traile flung himself down, firing as he dropped. The man behind the machine gun toppled to the floor of the truck. Another figure sprang to take his place, but the driver stopped him with a furious yell.

"You fool! We've got to get him alive!"

"It's too late!" The false servant had scrambled to his feet, blood streaming down his face. "Beat it! G-men!"

A taxi was thundering down the street from the direction of Fifth Avenue. In a hurried side-glance, Traile saw two of Allen's agents on the running boards. With frantic haste, the Invisible Emperor's spies jumped into the speed-truck and fled. Traile stood up, pumped two shots at the rear of the machine, but it raced on and was quickly swallowed up in traffic.

A robed form came into view—it was Doctor Yen Sin!

"Let it go!" Traile exclaimed, as one of the agents shot a hasty question at him. "I need your help inside."

He had left the library door open, and when he and the first of the squad entered they found the three victims beginning to stir. Traile and the others carried them out into the hall, and they soon revived. Bannister was the first one able to speak.

"What the devil happened?"

"We walked into a neat trap," Traile said with a slight note of curtness. "Kent had been dead hours before we got here—but Yen Sin twisted it to his advantage and nearly won."

Ten minutes later, the entire group returned to the library for a final examination of the scene while they waited for the police. Suddenly a clicking sounded from the micro-set which Traile had laid on the table. Then, to his astonishment, the voice of the Yellow Doctor spoke.

"I congratulate you, Mr. Traile, but you have only delayed our meeting."

There was a hush as the assembled men stared at the miniature radio. Then the sibilant voice of Yen Sin continued.

"And to Citizen Nine, I give this final message: You have until midnight to live!"

CHAPTER 8
MURDER GARDEN

NIGHT HAD fallen over Manhattan. From the roof of the towering Hotel Lordmore, the vast expanse of lighted streets below was pleasantly remote, a picturesque background for Mark Bannister's sumptuous penthouse.

Along the stone guard-wall at one end of the roof, Michael

Traile stood with a field glass raised to his eyes. The millionaire paced restlessly back and forth beside him.

"It's after ten," Bannister grated out. "If Allen's coming up with more men, why isn't he here?"

Traile did not seem to have heard him. He moved the glass slowly over the twinkling lights on the East River, on out toward the Sound, then back to the nearest skyscraper.

"An excellent view," he said as he put down the glass.

"To hell with the view!" exploded the millionaire. "Do you realize I'm likely to go like Kent and poor old Courtland?"

"I don't think you need worry," Traile said calmly. "This place is almost impregnable."

Bannister stared back through the gloom, to where Eric Gordon and two F.B.I. men stood near the brightly lighted penthouse.

"That's what I thought," he muttered. "But from all you've told me, this Doctor Yen Sin must be almost superhuman. And now that Cloyd has disappeared—"

He shook his head gloomily.

Traile turned a moment later, as Eric quickly approached them.

"Your elevator signal is buzzing," Eric said to Bannister.

Bannister strode toward the penthouse. Traile and Eric followed him through a Japanese gate, one of the curios the millionaire had brought back from the East. It opened into a walled Oriental garden, partly roofed and rather flamboyantly blending Chinese and Japanese motifs. A pale purple moon shone dimly on a tiny arched bridge, under which ran an artificial brook. Back in the shadows stood a pagoda-shaped shrine. Colored lanterns, farther on, illuminated an open display of Samurai swords, Chinese highbinder hatchets, and other Oriental weapons of a past day.

The millionaire scowled about him as he stalked through the garden.

"This place is going to be changed. After today, I don't want anything Chinese around me!"

"I don't blame you," said Eric. "Even the sight of a Chink laundryman gives me the jitters now."

In the large reception hall, Bannister stopped before his private switchboard. He spoke into a phone, listened, then turned a knob marked *Elevator*.

"It's Allen and his men," he grunted.

Traile's dark eyes were watching the indicator. The car came up swiftly, stopped automatically. Bannister peered through the observation panel, touched the release which opened the double doors. Allen and the operative named Johnson stepped out. Bannister frowned.

"Where are the rest of your men?"

The lanky senior agent shrugged.

"Helping the cops search Chinatown. After Weller phoned me about the layout up here, I didn't think we'd need any more."

The millionaire glowered at him. Allen rubbed his jaw, looked around curiously.

"Weller said the elevator is the only way to get up here. I guess this job's a cinch."

"I told him there was also an emergency exit," snapped

Bannister. He pointed to a heavy door with massive double locks. "However, it can be opened only from this side, and there's a similar door—locked the same way—at the bottom of the steps. It opens into the hall of the floor below. Both doors are connected with these burglar-alarm bells on the switchboard."

Allen nodded, glanced at Traile.

"I guess we won't see the Yellow Doctor tonight…. By the way, here's your gun. You left it at the Kent place."

Bannister gave Traile a sour look. "A lot of help you'd have been, if anything had happened while we were driving to the hotel tonight. They might have kidnapped me—and I'd probably have died like Harley Kent."

Traile inspected the magazine of the .38, slid it back into the butt.

"In that case," he said, "you would have died very quickly."

"It's plain he was tortured," snapped the millionaire. "How do you know how he died?"

"I should know," Traile said coolly. "I was the one who killed him."

Bannister took a step backward.

"*You?*" he rasped. Then the angry glare returned to his eyes. "This is no time for jokes!"

"I'm not joking," said Traile. He looked at Eric and Johnson, who were staring at him in amazement. Then he turned back to the millionaire. "I killed him in self-defense. Harley Kent was the Gray Man I shot at the Courtland mansion."

Bannister looked from him to Allen. The senior agent nodded.

"That's right. The slug found in Kent's heart tallied exactly in rifling marks with a test bullet fired from that .38."

"But I don't understand," Bannister said dazedly.

"It's quite simple," Traile told him. "They were attempting to cover up the truth. From the medical examiner's report, Kent's body must have been brought to his home soon after the Gray Men escaped from the Courtland place. They bound it as you saw, then stabbed it with a red-hot poker, also plunging the iron into the bullet hole in his left side so it would look like the other wounds. Either they forgot the bullet in their haste, or they had no means of probing for it."

"But—Harley Kent, a criminal!" Bannister exclaimed. "Why, it's impossible!"

Traile's deep-tanned face was stern.

"He was evidently driven to it by desperation. If I'm right, the Gray Men are rich and influential victims of the Yellow Doctor. Perhaps one or two are willing members, actuated by greed in joining the Invisible Empire. But I think most of them have been trapped by blackmail or some other insidious scheme, and then forced to do Yen Sin's bidding."

The millionaire looked horrified.

"Then that's what he intended to do with me!"

"It looks that way," Traile said grimly.

"What about the gray faces of those men?" put in Agent Johnson. "You think they were made up, like that girl this morning?"

Eric Gordon winced. Traile shook his head.

"Nothing that complicated. I believe they wear some kind

of thin rubber masks which conform partly with their real features, yet conceal their identity. That adhesive tape on Kent's mouth gave me a hint. I found sticky spots where something had adhered to his face. I thought of a mask, and that fitted in with what I noticed about that wound. They must wear the masks so they will be able to distinguish each other when they're carrying out some mission, and still be disguised from other members of the Invisible Empire—perhaps even from one another."

"The thing's fantastic," Bannister said incredulously. "What possible good could it do this Invisible Emperor?"

As Traile replied he led the way out to the unlighted sun deck.

"Getting them more deeply involved would be the initial reason. I suspect that he's building toward some tremendous goal, and he wants to get those men completely in his power so that they can't rebel at the last. But whatever it is, the stakes are sure to be enormous."

Allen savagely bit off the end of a cigar.

"After what happened to Jim Stone, I'd like just one minute with that yellow fiend!"

HE SCRATCHED a match on the guard-wall. Bannister jumped nervously at the sound. Allen paused with the blazing match half-raised to his cigar.

"By the way, where're Murdock and Weller?"

"On the other side," volunteered Eric.

"Let's go around there," said Allen.

As they started along the dark walk by the guard-wall, the

musical sound of chimes came from somewhere in the penthouse.

"Eleven o'clock!" Bannister said in a strained voice. "By God, I'm going in where it's light!"

He wheeled back along the sun deck, but he had not taken four steps when a voice rose in a shout from the other side of the roof.

"Help! Something's happened to Weller!"

Traile whirled to Eric Gordon and Allen.

"You two stay here with Bannister!"

Johnson snapped on a flashlight as he ran after Traile.

"Hold it out to the side," Traile flung over his shoulder.

The light swerved and, as they reached the Japanese gate, fell on the chunky figure of Agent Murdock. The man's round face had a stunned expression.

"This way!" he jerked out hoarsely.

They followed him through the garden. Beyond the little arched bridge Murdock halted, pointing dumbly to the floor. Kneeling there before the shrine, bent over with his forehead to a prayer mat, was Weller. His face, as seen from the side, was the color of old parchment.

Traile shot a swift look backward, then stooped over the silent figure. The man did not move as he touched him. He grasped the agent's shoulder, shook it. Weller toppled over sidewise, his body rigidly retaining its queer, kneeling pose.

"He's dead!" gasped Johnson.

Traile wheeled, took the flashlight, and swept it about the garden.

"Did you see it happen?" he demanded of Murdock.

Before Murdock could answer, Bannister and the others appeared from the direction of the sun deck. Eric Gordon and Allen were trying to keep the millionaire back. But he pulled away from them.

"I insist on knowing what—" He broke off as he saw the queerly rigid body. "My God, he's been killed!"

"Weller!" groaned Allen. He sprang forward, but Traile stopped him.

"Wait! Don't touch him yet." He probed the flashlight around again, then turned quickly to Bannister. "Those colored lanterns don't help much. Switch on some bright lights."

Bannister shook his head.

"The lanterns are the only ones connected in the garden."

Traile bent for a hasty scrutiny of Weller's body. Then, at his direction, Murdock and Johnson carried the dead agent into the reception hall. He closed the glass door to the garden, handed Allen the flashlight.

"Keep it pointed at that door. Eric, you and Johnson watch toward the sides of the roof. Fire at anything that moves."

"I thought you searched this place," Alien muttered.

"We did," Traile said grimly. He looked at Murdock. "Now, let's hear what you know."

The man tore his eyes away from the grotesquely stiffened form on the floor.

"I thought he was somewhere near me. He'd been wandering around in the garden. Then I heard something buzz, like a bee, right close to my ear. It gave me a start, and I began looking for Weller. When I found him he was bent down in front of that heathen shrine, just like he was praying. He was shaking as though he was scared to death, and he wouldn't say a word. That's when I yelled for help."

ALLEN TOOK his gaze from the glass door for a brief stare at the dead man. "He must've had some kind of fit. But I never heard of rigor mortis setting in so fast."

Traile motioned to Bannister. "Help me turn him over."

The millionaire recoiled.

"I wouldn't even touch him! You can't tell what killed him."

"I can guess," Traile said shortly. He turned the dead agent onto his back. Weller's head was still bent, and his limbs rigidly fixed in their curious position. Traile looked at the wildly dilated eyes, then pointed to a small brown spot under Weller's jaw.

"There's the answer. A tiny dart or needle went in there. That smear is *lakta*, a Malay poison. There's enough left on the outside to stop a full-grown tiger."

As he stood up the others looked at him with horror.

"Then that buzz I heard—" Murdock said, ashen-faced.

"Was either that dart—or another one meant for you," Traile finished.

Bannister suddenly turned and closed the door to the sun deck.

"Leave it open," Traile said quickly.

"You're crazy!" rasped the millionaire. "The dart must have been shot from the top of that office building across the street. They may shoot another at any second."

"None of Yen Sin's killers are on top of that building," snapped Traile. "The danger is here on this roof."

"Then why are you standing here idle?" stormed Bannister. He made a furious gesture. "You've bungled it from start to finish—had me get rid of my bodyguards—refused to call in the police—"

Traile went after him as he spun around toward his private telephone.

"What are you going to do?"

"Get some real protection up here!" snarled Bannister. "You've let one man be murdered, and I'm likely to be the next!"

"You will be," Trails said sharply, "if you try to send that signal!"

Bannister froze, glaring down at Traile's leveled gun.

"Hare you lost your senses?" he said hoarsely.

Traile's dark eyes drilled into the other man s face.

"The game's up, Bannister. You're a good actor—but not good enough."

The millionaire tamed a chalky white.

""You're stark mad!" he cried. "Grab his gun, one of you!"

Johnson jumped toward Traile, but Allen halted him with a brusque command. Traile searched the millionaire, handed a Mannlicher pistol to Eric.

"Keep him covered. Don't let him get near that switchboard. He'd signal Yen Sin's agents down in the hotel—and there may be two or three dozen of them planted in different rooms, waiting to come up here."

Eric's blue eyes were wide with astonishment.

91

"Then he's really a member of the Invisible Empire?"

""Probably its chief agent in New York," Traile answered. The attack in Lexington Avenue was a fake. Doctor Yen Sin deliberately sacrificed those Chinese gunmen for effect, so that Bannister wouldn't be suspected while he helped to recover the gold skull."

"I tell you you're crazy," fumed the millionaire. "I never heard of him until today—except as the 'Cobra.'"

A cold smile lighted Traile's lean face.

"The secret reports and those other half-truths were clever business, Bannister—but you gave yourself away when you played the role of the Gray Man. You see, while you were unconscious at Kent's home, I found one of the rubber gloves you wore as a Gray Man. Later Allen turned the glove inside out and took the fingerprints. They matched perfectly with those on the report you'd been handling."

Murderous fury leaped into the other man's eyes.

"I knew I should have killed you!"

Traile motioned with the .38.

"Turn around. Face the wall and keep your hands up against it."

Bannister obeyed with an oath. Traile stepped back close to Allen, took from his pocket what appeared to be a thick toy pistol.

"Use this on him if you have to," he whispered. He put the miniature gun on a stand by the F.B.I. man. "We don't want to shoot him. I'm almost positive he's Yen Sin's key man in New

York, and if we can make him talk we'll wipe the Invisible Empire off the map."

Allen had his left hand partway out of his coat pocket. He dropped whatever he had been about to withdraw.

"Then you're not ready for—"

"Not yet," Traile said in an undertone. "It's clear that one of the Yellow Doctor's assassins has been smuggled onto the roof. I think I know where he's hiding."

"Then take Murdock and Johnson and go after him," Allen said hastily.

"No, you don't know those devils. If he found he was trapped, he'd be sure to get one or two of us before he died. I've a plan for nabbing him. Give me a minute or so to steal around on the sun-deck side, and get near the gate. Then turn the flashlight away from the garden."

"All right," Allen agreed reluctantly. "But for Heaven's sake be careful."

With a final glance about him, Traile stepped through the door at his right and was soon hidden in the shadows. He had left the flashlight pointed toward the garden so that no one could see beyond it and observe his departure. He tiptoed along in the darkness, with his gun poised for a quick shot. His movements had the stealth of a stalking tiger.

He paused until his eyes were accustomed to the gloom, then went on toward the gate. He was moving now with infinite caution, making sure of each deep shadow. The glow from the flashlight shone through from the other end of the garden. He stopped, crouched down by the gate, waiting for the light to be shifted.

It was turned away in a few seconds, and he could see through the glass door at the farther end. Bannister was still facing the paneled wall, with Eric covering him. Allen and his two men were looking nervously about them. Only the dim light of the colored lanterns shone in the garden.

It was then that Traile noticed that the artificial moon had been turned off. He edged past the gate, moved silently toward the shrine. Within a few feet of it he suddenly halted. Was it imagination, or had a faint sound come from the shadows near the display of Oriental weapons?

He crouched at one side of the shrine, staring toward the spot. A minute passed. He heard Bannister's angry voice, muffled by the glass door, and Allen's curt response. Then silence again, a silence which grew more tense with every passing second.

From somewhere in the penthouse the sweet, musical sound of the chimes was audible again. Bannister at once burst into another angry protest. And in that moment the shrine began to move!

Traile sprang back, flattened himself against the decorated wall of the garden. His suspicion was right. The chimes were a signal to Bannister, controlled from the hiding place of the assassin.

Pivoting at one corner, the shrine swung open on noiseless hinges. Traile held his breath, for it was the side next to him which had swung away from the wall. Motionless, he waited, almost as dark as the shadow where he stood. As the shrine ceased to move, his finger took up the slack of his trigger.

No one appeared. Traile strained his eyes to pierce the darkness back of the shrine. Finally a faint *pat-pat* came to his ears, accompanied by a low, swishing sound. A shadowy figure seemed to rise from out of the floor. Traile—watched in brief amazement, then the truth burst on him.

The shrine had concealed a secret stairway to a room on the floor below.

The man ascending the stairs was almost at the top, when, to Traile's dismay, whispering voices sounded from below. The full peril of the situation struck him like a blow. A dozen of the Yellow Doctor's spies must be coming up those steps.

Before he could hurl himself against the shrine, a robed form came into view. Traile's pulses gave a leap.

It was Doctor Yen Sin!

CHAPTER 9
THE THREE HATCHETS

TRAILE SPRANG and rammed his gun against the Yellow Doctor's side, forcing him to block the narrow opening.

"Don't move!" he said fiercely.

For just an instant, fear showed in the Satanic face before him. Then the cold mockery came back to Yen Sin's eyes.

"So you decided to hasten our meeting, Mr. Traile?"

A low, metallic clink sounded from the other side of the

garden. Traile half-whirled, trying to watch both directions. There stood a glaring Chinese with a hatchet!

As the man's arm whipped forward, Traile desperately hurled himself sidewise. The hatchet buried itself in the shrine, just beyond his shoulder.

There was a rush of feet, and three men leaped from the stairway as Yen Sin stepped aside. Already off balance, Traile was thrown to the floor. A hand gripped his throat, cutting off his attempt at a shout. He jerked the gun toward the man's head, but it was wrenched away.

As he was held down, one of the men hastily taped his mouth. Two more twisted his arms, then brought him to his feet at the Crime Emperor's low-spoken command. He looked hopefully toward the penthouse door, but Bannister was still haranguing furiously and the muffled sounds of that silent battle had gone unheard.

Doctor Yen Sin calmly surveyed the scene beyond the glass door, from his vantage point in the gloom. Then he turned, spoke in a low tone to a sallow-skinned Eurasian. The half-caste went back toward the secret stairway, reappeared with a girl. As she tore herself free from the man's grasp, Traile recognized the beautiful face of Sonya Damitri. The Yellow Doctor fixed his weird eyes on her.

"You will go with Kang Fu, and do as I instructed."

She turned, hopelessly, with the Eurasian and two more spies closely following. They disappeared to the left of the arched bridge. Doctor Yen Sin nodded to the men holding Traile.

"To the right," he said in whispered Chinese. "And move exactly as I ordered."

Twisting his arms so that he was forced to walk on tiptoe, Traile's captors marched him toward the side of the penthouse. As they neared the door to the reception hall, he saw Allen looking anxiously around the room. Eric had Bannister covered, but the millionaire's head was twisted around and he was snarling something over his shoulder.

There was a sudden crash from the dim-lit garden. Allen jumped toward the glass door, and his two agents raced after him. Instantly, Traile's captors plunged into the hall with him, and at the same moment Sonya appeared from the sun-deck side, two armed men crouching back of her.

Eric had whirled as the two doors burst open. He jerked his gun toward the left, then stood paralyzed at sight of Sonya. Bannister was on him in a flash. He snatched at the Mannlicher, and in a moment both men were on the floor, struggling for the gun.

Allen and the two agents had spun around at the first sound of action. After an instant of amazement, Murdock sprang at the men holding Traile. Something buzzed by Traile's shoulder, and a dark spot appeared on Murdock's cheek. The agent jerked to a stop, his eyes bulging. His lips opened convulsively, then his knees buckled and he fell to the floor.

The glass door was swiftly flung open, and three Burmese dacoits leaped at Allen and Johnson. With an ape-like jump, one of the thugs hurled himself onto Johnson's back. The agent went down with the dacoit's fingers locked around his throat. His head struck the floor with a thump, and he ceased to move.

The two other thugs seized Allen before he could turn. His right arm was wrenched around behind him with bone-breaking force. He groaned, let his pistol fall. With despair, Traile saw that Bannister had gained possession of the Mannlicher. Eric was writhing on the floor from a vicious blow to the groin.

As the millionaire jumped up, there was momentary silence. Then from the shadows of the garden, Doctor Yen Sin slowly came forward. He glanced around the room without emotion, turned to Bannister.

"If you had followed instructions," he said icily, "this would not have been necessary."

Bannister had a frightened look.

"I didn't have a chance. Traile was onto me."

The Yellow Doctor smiled contemptuously.

"I am afraid you lack in courage, my friend."

"I'm in a spot," the millionaire said harshly. "He guessed the truth this morning. They've probably got agents here in the building, ready to grab me."

"They will not trouble you," replied Doctor Yen Sin. He looked sardonically at Allen. "You should have advised at least some of your men not to ask for rooms on the topmost floors."

Allen lunged at him.

"You yellow devil! What have you done with them?"

His captors hauled him back. The Crime Emperor regarded him without expression, then turned.

"And you, Mr. Traile—I gave you credit for more ingenuity."

Traile met his gaze coolly. Doctor Yen Sin looked at his taped lips, beckoned to Traile's guards.

"Bring him closer." When they had obeyed, he fixed his strange, tawny eyes on Traile's face. "I shall not insult your intelligence by any pretense about your eventual end. But I shall make it more swift in exchange for certain information."

He signaled to the Eurasian who had used Sonya as a shield.

"Kang Fu, assist Mr. Traile to speak."

The half-caste approached with an ugly grin. Traile set his jaw. Kang Fu reached out, brutally ripped away the tape. It was like a fiery lash across Traile's lips, but he made no sound. Doctor Yen Sin gave him a thin smile.

"An heroic display of bravery, Mr. Traile. And now, the first question. What is the drug which enables you to go without sleep for so long?"

Traile made no answer. The Yellow Doctor frowned, then nodded to the men holding him. They forced Traile against the wall, twisting his arms until it seemed they would be torn from their sockets. Drops of perspiration stood out on his forehead. He saw Sonya close her eyes, shuddering. A red-hot agony shot through his ever-wakeful brain. Then, abruptly, that torturing pull was relaxed.

"He would faint before he would speak," he heard Yen Sin mutter. "Hold him there. We will try another way."

Eric Gordon had almost recovered from Bannister's cruel blow. As he staggered to his feet, the Crime Emperor gestured curtly to the millionaire.

"Keep him back." He turned, whispered to the Chinese whom

Traile had seen in the garden. The man disappeared, came back quickly. In spite of himself, Traile started as he saw the three hatchets the Chinese carried.

"I see you have heard of this ceremony," Doctor Yen Sin said with ironic amusement. "Perhaps you are ready to answer the first question?"

Traile's eyes shifted for an instant to Allen. The F.B.I. man was looking helplessly toward the door to the darkened sun deck. Yen Sin quickly followed Traile's glance, but Allen was now staring at the floor. The Yellow Doctor motioned to the waiting hatchet man. Eric burst out with a cry as the Chinese took his position.

"Tell him, Michael, for God's sake!"

"It would do no good," said Traile, grimly.

HIS CAPTORS drew away on each side, still holding his arms twisted so that he was forced against the wall. He felt them tense as the Chinese drew back the first hatchet.

"One," said Doctor Yen Sin.

The hatchet man's arm shot forward. With a savage swish, the weapon dashed toward Traile. For an instant it seemed aimed straight between his eyes. Then it whirled past and thudded into the wall an inch from his head. The quivering handle almost touched his ear.

The Crime Emperor looked at him with slitted eyes.

"Now, are you ready to speak?"

Before Traile had time to reply, Eric recklessly leaped past Bannister and struck at Traile's nearest guard.

"Get back!" Traile groaned. "They'll only kill you, too."

Kang Fu and a dacoit seized Eric, pulled him away. Doctor Yen Sin gazed shrewdly from Traile to Eric.

"I perceive a swifter means for my purpose," he said to the millionaire.

At his brief order, Traile was hustled to one side, and Eric pinioned against the wall in his place. Sonya Damitri ran toward Yen Sin, but he thrust her aside. She turned wildly to Traile.

"You brought him into this! Save him, while there is yet time."

The Crime Emperor's yellow face darkened.

"I will have no more of your maudlin sympathy for this young American!" He gave a command, and a ferocious-looking Burmese dragged the girl out of the way. Then he turned to Traile. "Her suggestion, however, is the one I intended to make. I will free him when it is safe—if you answer my two questions. The first one you know. The second: What are the names of the other Q-men?"

Traile faced him stonily.

"I'll tell you, if you include Allen and Johnson—and swear by the bones of your ancestors that you'll free them."

Yen Sin's brows drew together, then he looked around at Allen and the unconscious agent on the floor.

"I agree," he said, shortly. "But they will not be liberated in this country."

"Very well," Traile said. "Then here are your answers. There is no drug—I can't sleep because of an accident. And there are no other Q-men."

The concussion came through the water like a sudden blow.

The Yellow Doctor stiffened, then the pupils of his queer eyes dilated with a violent passion.

"Do you expect me to believe such childish lies?" He whirled to the hatchet man, pointed at Eric. "Finish your work!"

"Wait!" Traile cried. "I've told you the truth!"

But the second hatchet was already whizzing through the

air. Sonya screamed, and Traile turned cold with fear. Then, with a tremendous surge of relief, he saw that Eric fortunately had not tried to dodge. The hatchet had half-buried itself in the paneled wall, so that now the two handles kept his head from moving.

Yen Sin turned a look of icy hate on Traile.

"A last chance! Answer—or the third hatchet goes squarely between the others!"

Eric's boyish face was white, but his lips were trying to smile.

"All right!" Trails said desperately. "I'll tell you! Here in the back of my wristwatch… a supply of the capsules…."

YEN SIN'S tawny eyes lit with an eager flame. At his sharp command, the dacoit at Traile's right loosened his grasp to unstrap the watch. Traile jerked his arm free, swung with all his might at the man on his left. The thug's head snapped back from the blow, and Traile dived madly for the toylike gun on the stand. The first dacoit plunged after him with a snarl of fury. Traile snatched up the miniature weapon, but the Burmese was on him before he could touch the trigger. Three more of Yen Sin's agents were racing to the spot. Traile slammed his fist into the dacoit's throat. As the man's clawing hands fell away, he pressed the stubby trigger.

Zip! A cartridge of tear-gas concentrate burst against the wall. The steamy vapor almost instantly filled the room. Traile had frantically rolled to one side as he fired the tear-gas gun. He could dimly see two of Yen Sin's men pile over the one he had crippled.

He jumped up, trying to find Allen. Pandemonium had

broken loose behind him. Suddenly, a hazy figure bumped against him. A wild blow scraped along his shoulder, and he heard the other man curse. "Allen!" he rapped out.

"Where's the doorway?" the agent said thickly.

Above the clamor, Yen Sin's choked voice rose with a note of rage. Traile pushed Allen in the other direction. He heard the door being opened, felt cool air on his face. The senior agent stumbled outside. He was about to follow when a vague figure lunged into view. There was a gun in the man's extended hand. He sprang, tore the weapon away. The man struck blindly at him, missed. Traile landed a left hook, sent him reeling backward.

Three shrill blasts of a whistle sounded from outside on the roof. They were echoed almost at once from somewhere near. Trail dashed through the doorway, leaped to one side. A fan of white light was spreading from the top of the building diagonally across the street. It flashed toward the hotel roof, then the whistle blasts were drowned by the piercing shriek of a siren.

CHAPTER 10
DEATH TRAP

THREE OR four staggering figures were brilliantly outlined in the glare which swept the garden. One of the spies dashed his hand across his streaming eyes. When he caught sight of a man crouching down by the guard wall, he fiercely lifted his arm. Traile fired as he saw the man's raised hatchet.

The Chinese lurched back, and the weapon dropped from his hand. He doubled over and fell. At the same moment Allen's whistle shrilled another signal. From behind the floodlight, a tommy gun began to chatter. The spies back of the hatchet man wilted to the floor.

As the tommy gun ceased to pound, the siren on the office building roof lessened its piercing shriek. From four directions, down in the streets of Manhattan, that shriek was quickly answered. Traile plunged back into the penthouse. The tear gas was being sucked out toward the garden, and he could now see the spot where Eric had stood. The two hatchets still protruded from the wall, but there was no sign of the young Southerner.

He stumbled over Murdock's body, felt his way toward the glass door. Panicky voices were audible from the direction of the elevator. He ran toward it, but the doors had clicked shut. Through the steamy whiteness of the tear gas, the observation panel was visible. He dimly saw the group which had crowded into the car. Eric was struggling in the hands of Kang Fu and Bannister. In front of Sonya and two Asian spies stood Doctor Yen Sin.

Traile leaped toward the switchboard, but the car was starting to move and the special switch had no effect. He had a last glimpse of the Crime Emperor's malignant face, then the car dropped from sight. He dashed out onto the roof. Allen was shouting through cupped hands at the squad of F.B.I. men over on the other building.

"Come on!" Traile broke in. "They've escaped and taken Eric!"

They ran past the bullet-torn gate. The dying hatchet man

cursed them in Chinese as they hurried by. Traile turned to the shrine.

"Why not the emergency doors?" exclaimed Allen.

"Bannister has the keys," clipped Traile. He poised the automatic, went down the narrow stairway, with Allen close behind. They emerged in one room of a special suite. A faint odor of incense was perceptible. The windows were closed and shuttered.

There were signs of hasty flight as they rushed through the other rooms, but no one was to be found. Traile led the way into the hall, just as more Federal agents with drawn guns appeared from the main elevators.

"Three of you stay up here—hunt for Clark's squad!" yelled Allen. "The rest of you come along!"

They ran to the first elevator. As it shot downward, Traile fired a query at the frightened operator.

"How many doors to the penthouse shaft?"

"Three beside the roof, sir," gasped the man. "Top floor, main, and the garage in the basement."

"Drop us all the way," rapped Traile. He looked at the leader of the squad. "Are the police closing in all right?"

"Yes, but I heard some shooting," the agent replied quickly.

When they reached the basement, they found a scene of wild confusion. An F.B.I. man dashed up to Allen, a bloody arm dangling.

"That Chinese and the bunch with him got away! They had a dozen men in cop's uniforms hidden around, and we got mixed up."

Traile ran toward the first car he saw, a big Duesenberg. Allen and three others tumbled in after him, and he sent the machine speeding up the ramp. As they reached the street, the senior agent called something to a policeman in a squad car. The police machine roared ahead, with Traile keeping close behind.

"They're heading toward the East River," Allen yelled above the howl of the sirens.

Traile grimly nodded.

"They'll probably make for Bannister's yacht on Long Island Sound."

THREE MINUTES later the cars halted by a small dock opposite Blackwell's Island. Nearby, a motorcycle man lay dead under his wrecked machine. Another officer, obviously wounded, ran toward them, cursing and groaning.

"They jumped on an express cruiser! They're going up the West Channel!"

A red-faced lieutenant ran for the nearest phone, but it was several minutes before a fast police boat swung in to the dock. Traile and the others jumped aboard, and the boat sped ahead in pursuit of the fleeing craft. As they approached Ward Island, the man at the searchlight gave an exclamation.

"There's a cruiser runnin' without lights!"

The darkened boat heeled to pass through the narrow channel. As it swung into the wider expanse of the East River, south of the Bronx, a green rocket flared up from the gloom beyond. It was answered by a red rocket from the commuting-cruiser. The searchlight man swerved the beam toward the spot from which the green signal had come. It fell on a trim white yacht some distance ahead.

"Hell!" he said, startled. "Why, that's the *Mahola*—Mark Bannister's yacht!"

"Keep your light on the cruiser," Traile said hurriedly. "They'll trick us if they get the chance."

After one attempt to dodge out of the beam, the commuter ploughed straight for the yacht. Traile frowned thoughtfully at the smaller craft.

"There's something odd about this," he muttered to Allen. "Even if we can't stop it, they must know that the yacht will be caught before it reaches open sea."

"Maybe we've been fooled," Allen said hastily. "They might not be aboard at all."

Traile looked at the searchlight man.

"Have you a pair of field glasses?"

"Right back of you," said the policeman.

Traile focused them on the cruiser. He could see several figures in the luxuriously-fitted cockpit at the stern. Doctor Yen Sin was looking back impassively. He saw Kang Fu, and he thought he glimpsed Eric lying helpless at the half-caste's feet. Bannister seemed to be arguing with the Crime Emperor. Yen Sin shook his head, turned, and vanished within the cabin.

"Don't let them out of your beam for a second," Traile said to the man at the searchlight "The most dangerous criminal alive is in that boat."

"You don't mean Bannister?" the cop gasped.

"No, but he's mixed up in it," said Traile.

"The yacht's lights are going on," exclaimed Allen.

Traile stared toward the vessel. Only the riding lights had

been showing. Now, lighted portholes made two strings of yellow dots along the yacht's side. Another light glowed, up on the bridge, then a powerful searchlight swept around toward the police boat. Traile shielded his eyes, tried to see ahead. In a moment the searchlight shifted, and he saw another police boat putting out from Flushing Bay. He raised the field glasses. Bannister and Doctor Yen Sin were now visible up in the deckhouse, as the cruiser slowed and turned in toward the *Mahola*. He saw Kang Fu and another man drag Eric to his feet.

The commuting-boat passed out of sight on the other side of the yacht. Traile put down the glasses, took out his pistol. Allen followed suit, and his agents made ready to board the yacht. It was almost two minutes before they reached the *Mahola*. The police boat quickly circled around to the starboard side, where the express cruiser rode at the gangway, empty.

Muffled voices could be heard aboard the yacht. Traile flung a warning to the agents and police as he jumped to the gangway.

"Be on guard every second! That devil's up to something. And watch out for the girl and a prisoner."

THE DECK was deserted. The boarding party spread out, covering port and starboard sides. Traile and Allen hastily searched the bridge, ran aft toward the main salon. The muffled voices seemed to come from below. There was a peculiar background of throbbing, metallic sounds which made the words and the source hard to determine.

Several of the others joined them as they stole down the main companionway. The dining saloon was as empty as the one above, but the voices were somewhat louder. Suddenly Traile heard Bannister's grating accents.

"But it cost me more than a million!"

"What are a few millions compared with all there is at stake?" came the calm retort of Doctor Yen Sin.

Traile ran silently into the passage aft of the dining saloon. As the others followed, Bannister's harsh voice was heard again in protest.

"I tell you this is madness! We'll be trapped like rats!"

"Traile and those others will be the ones to die," the Yellow Doctor's response sounded from behind a closed door. "After that, no one will guess the truth."

"You butcher!" Traile heard Eric Gordon cry out fiercely. "They'll get you some day for—"

The sound of a blow cut off his outburst. Traile motioned swiftly for the agents and police to group themselves at the sides of the door.

"Is the device ready?" Yen Sin's query came from inside.

"Not quite," said a nervous voice Traile did not recognize. "We want to be sure."

There was a sudden, high whine, like the whistle of a speaking tube. Then someone rasped a few indistinct words.

"What's the matter?" Traile heard Bannister demand.

"It's Fricht!" shrilled the man with the nervous voice. "The fool says he left his set on the—"

"Michael! Allen!" Eric's shout rang out behind the door. "For Heaven's sake get off—"

The words ended with a moan, then there was stark silence.

Traile seized the doorknob, jumped aside and flung open the door. The agents and police sprang forward with guns leveled. Then they stared at each other in blank amazement.

There was not a soul in the stateroom.

The red-faced lieutenant jumped inside, yanked open the only visible door. Nothing but a small closet was revealed. He kicked at the back of it, looked around in bewilderment.

"Where th' hell did they go? They couldn't have got out that porthole."

Traile gazed hurriedly around the stateroom. A box of long, black cigarettes lay on the lower bunk, near a small leather satchel like a man's overnight kit. He bent over the partly open satchel. For a moment he stared, puzzled, at its contents. Then a dismayed look flashed across his face and he whirled around.

"Get off the yacht as fast as you can!"

THERE WAS a hasty exodus from the stateroom. Traile snatched up the leather satchel and dashed after Allen.

"What is it?" the senior agent said breathlessly.

"No time to explain!" snapped Traile.

As the police charged out on deck, the alarmed coxswain started his engine. The officers and F.B.I. men tumbled down the gangway. While the last ones were still scrambling aboard, the coxswain started the boat ahead. Allen made a flying leap and landed on the gunwale.

"Hold on!" he bellowed. "There's one more man."

The distance was already too great for Traile to hurdle. He turned and raced toward the bow. Gripping the satchel, he jumped. The impact tore one of the handles from his grasp.

Before he could prevent it, the satchel opened and spilled its contents into the water. He let go of the bag, struck out toward the police boat. He was within twenty feet of it when a terrific explosion blasted the night.

The concussion, coming through the water, was like a sudden blow. The police boat rocked violently, and he saw several men thrown down. He dived to escape the heat of the blast, came up on the other side of the boat. As Allen helped him aboard he could partly make out the wrecked yacht through the glare of the flames.

The explosion had occurred amidships, and had practically blown the vessel apart. Even as he looked, he saw it break in two, and the blazing bow and stern sections begin to sink. He cast an anxious glance across the water.

"Where's the boat that came out from Flushing?"

A grizzled harbor policeman shook has head.

"They were lying close by the port side. I'm afraid they're done for."

"Poor devils," muttered Traile. He turned to the coxswain. "You'd better head for the darkest spot along shore. We may not be safe yet."

The boat swerved. Allen stared at Traile.

"But what could happen now? Yen Sin and his mob are at the bottom of the East River—what's left of them."

Traile gazed toward the sinking wreckage of the yacht. He slowly nodded.

"I still don't get all of it," Allen said. "I can see that Yen Sin and those others must have been behind some secret door in the stateroom. But what was he trying to do?"

Traile looked at the listening policemen. "He intended to finish us, but the scheme backfired," he replied briefly.

Allen shivered.

"That poor kid Gordon—and the girl! It's hard, their going like that. But at least we're rid of the Yellow Doctor."

The grizzled harbor man eyed Traile curiously.

"What gets me, how did you know it was goin' to happen?"

"I read the first lines of a message in that satchel," Traile answered. "That gave me the hint."

"Well, thank God for that!" said the policeman fervently.

But as he went forward, Traile drew Allen away from the other men.

"Can you stand a shock?" he said in an undertone.

"Huh?" said Allen. "What do you mean?"

"I want all the others to think that Doctor Yen Sin is dead."

Allen started.

"But, good Lord, he couldn't be alive! You yourself—"

"I admitted he was at the bottom of the East River. Unfortunately, he's very much alive. The *Mahola* was torpedoed."

"Torpedoed!" Allen whispered dazedly. Then he swore under his breath. "Jumping Jupiter! That lost-submarine business that's been in all the papers!"

"Exactly," Traile said in a grim voice. "I read about it myself, and never even suspected. But it's a perfect means of escape for Yen Sin, if he's too closely pressed."

"I see it now," Allen said savagely. "Bannister's a director of the Lodin Submarine Corporation. He worked it so that a bunch of crooks were in the crew on the test runs, and they took command by force."

"And they've simply been hiding somewhere, or lying submerged in the daytime," assented Traile, "getting signals from Yen Sin or Bannister. Tonight, they evidently came up on the other side of the yacht and took off everyone from the express cruiser. Then they submerged to the periscope, eased off a little way in the dark, and waited until we were on board the yacht before firing the torpedo."

"But how the devil did you get wise?" Allen queried.

"The man called Fricht was evidently on the yacht to maintain communication with the sub and with Dr. Yen Sin. That satchel contained a compact two-way radio. There was an extension cord for plugging in the transmitter, but the receiver was already switched on. Fricht must have left it that way in his hurry to escape."

"So that's how we heard them!" interjected Allen. Then he added excitedly: "We can still capture them. With your Navy connection, you can get some destroyers out in the Sound—they could drop nets or depth bombs, and bottle the sub up—"

Traile gravely shook his head.

"Eric is a prisoner, and I'm going to save him if it's humanly possible. Yen Sin will think he's safe now. He'll hide out for a day or two to make sure, and then shift to some base in New York. He won't give up this mysterious scheme of his, you can bank on that."

"I believe you're right," Allen said quickly. "He wouldn't have built up that group of Gray Men and all his spy system, unless he was after something big."

"Today's events, with that desperate business about the Golden Skull, prove that." Traile gazed soberly across the water toward the distant skyline of Manhattan. "Allen, I've a feeling that we haven't heard the last of the *Chuen Gin Lou.*"

CHAPTER 11
THE HONG KONG CHEST

OUTSIDE THE Q-Station, purple dusk was settling over the city, but within Michael Traile's heavily curtained den the lights were blazing. Traile stood before the wall map of Greater New York, his eyes on the area known as Chinatown. There was weariness in the pose of his tall figure. The bronze of his face had paled somewhat from long hours spent indoors.

He turned restlessly, went into the adjoining room. His glance passed over Eric Gordon's bed, and the sad look in his eyes deepened. It had been four days since Eric had vanished as a prisoner of Doctor Yen Sin. He slid back the panel which covered the special telephone system that Eric had installed. One of the lines was a direct wire to his contact officer at the Brooklyn Navy Yard. He plugged the connection.

"Q-four," he said, when a voice answered. "Any further report from the patrol?"

"Not a thing, sir," the officer replied. "I'm afraid they got away."

"Hold to the same schedule," said Traile. He disconnected,

was about to make another call when his door buzzer rasped. He went to the vestibule, glanced up at the mirror which was placed to show whoever was outside. It was Allen.

"I was about to call you," he said as he admitted the F.B.I. man. A hopeful look replaced his weariness as he saw the excited expression on the lanky agent's face. "What's happened?" he asked.

"It's not about Eric, I'm sorry to say," Allen responded. "But I'll bet my shirt it's connected with Yen Sin."

Traile closed the steel-backed door. Allen was hastily taking an X-ray film from a large manila envelope.

"It's got me going in circles," he exclaimed. "This was just one of several routine jobs done in the last three days. It was an exposure made of an ordinary document we suspected of being a forgery. But here's what we found!"

He lifted the shade from a table lamp and held the film close to the light. Traile leaned down, stared at the X-ray picture. The typewritten words of the document stood out clearly against a blurred but terrible background. A diabolical face looked out from behind the legal lettering, a face like some hideous thing seen in a nightmare. It had no ears, and its lips were stretched wide so that the teeth showed from jaw to jaw. The eyes were two slits of staring horror, and the lower part of the nose had been cut away.

"Good Heaven!" Traile whispered.

"I damn near fell out of my chair when I saw it," Allen said. "Then I realized it was a picture of some poor guy that had been tortured. Right away I thought of Doctor Yen Sin—"

He started, for Traile had snatched the film and was bending over it feverishly.

"I got men after the bird we think forged it," he began, but Traile cut him short.

"We'll have to go to your office! My microscope outfit is in Washington."

"But what's the idea?" said Allen, blankly.

Without answering, Traile held the film almost against the lamp. The face was still blurred, and the close-spaced lines of the document obscured much of the detail, but he could catch the general effect. The cheeks were shrunken, and the emptiness of the eyes was more horrible than it had seemed at first. The forehead, where the legal writing did not cover it, was marked with a mass of tiny blurred scratches or cuts, suggestive of slow, deliberate torture.

"Hellish!" Traile muttered as he straightened up. "Only one man in the world would ever have thought of it."

"What I don't see," said Allen, "is why or how it was ever printed on that paper. It must have been done with invisible ink, of course, but what idea could they—"

HE STOPPED as Traile laid down the film and went rummaging through a pile of newspaper clippings on his desk. In a moment Traile returned with the photograph of a gaunt, elderly man. He penciled the eyes to a solid blackness, blocked out the ears and altered the mouth and nose. As he held it up beside the film, Allen jumped. Then he stared at the name under the photograph.

"Holy mackerel! It's John J. Meredith—the broker who disappeared two weeks ago."

Traile's dark eyes held a strange light.

"It's part of the answer, Allen! We should have seen it before."

He put the film and the clipping into the envelope.

"Look here," said Allen aggrievedly, "if you've figured out something, you might—"

They both turned at the sound of the buzzer. Traile stepped to the door, glanced up at the angled mirror. With a puzzled look, he beckoned to Allen. The F.B.I. man stared up into the glass. The reflection showed a tall Hong Kong chest, beautifully carved, standing on end just outside the door. There was no one in sight.

"How many people know about that X-ray?" Traile whispered.

"Only myself and Griel—the assistant lab man who took Stone's place," Allen replied. "But why?"

"It couldn't be that, then," Traile said, as though to himself. He pushed a wall-switch button, and a bright light outside shone down on the carved chest. Several Chinese characters, painted on the lid, were at once discernible. The mirror reversed them, and it took Traile a few seconds to read the short inscription. Suddenly he turned pale, sprang to unlock the door.

"Watch your step," Allen said tensely. "It may be a trick to bump you off."

But Traile heedlessly ran out, and with shaking hands unfastened the brass clamps of the long lid. It swung open like a door. A broken cry came to his lips as he looked inside. Within the chest was a stiffened form, held upright by three web belts.

And the white, waxen face which showed in the light was the face of Eric Gordon!

"My God!" groaned Allen. "They've killed him."

Traile, after his first short cry, made no other sound. He reached out one hand, touched the pale cheek of that pitiful figure. It was as cold as marble. Like a man in a stupor, he turned to Allen.

"We must—take him—inside," he said dully.

They closed the lid, laid the chest flat, and then carried it into the second room. Without a word, Traile unfastened the belts. He shook his head as Allen bent to help him. Unaided, he lifted Eric's body and laid it upon the bed. For more than a minute he stood looking down at the cold white face.

"Eric!" he whispered. "Eric…."

Allen's eyes blurred. But after a moment he touched Traile's arm.

"You can't let it get you like this. He wouldn't want you to—" He stopped, pointed down. "Look, there's something in his left hand."

TRAILE GENTLY pried apart the stiff fingers. The object was a small glass bottle with a paper rolled up inside. He removed the paper, saw that it was a message in Chinese. Dull anger, then a sudden wild hope, came into his eyes as he read. He whirled toward the den. Allen followed, stared in amazement as Traile switched on his microwave set and fumbled with the dial.

"What's up?" he asked in a startled voice, but the taller man was now springing to the window. A few minutes after Traile

119

threw back the heavy curtains, a low hum became audible from the miniature radio. Then a mocking voice spoke.

"I am sorry, Mr. Traile, to have caused you these moments of grief."

Traile's face was stony, but Allen flushed with rage.

"It's Yen Sin!" he rasped.

Traile motioned him to keep silent.

"You will tilt your desk lamp so that it shines directly on your face," the voice of the Yellow Doctor went on silkily. Then, as Traile obeyed, "That is better... stand back a little farther, if you please."

"For God's sake, Traile, are you crazy?" Allen burst out "He'll kill you!"

"The glass is bulletproof," Traile muttered over his shoulder.

"Keep your face toward the window," came the sharpened accents of Doctor Yen Sin. "And for Mr. Allen's benefit, it will do no good to take a bearing on this station. It will be moved within five minutes."

Allen let out an explosive gasp. There was a pause, then the suave voice continued.

"As you probably have guessed, Mr. Traile, you are being observed through binoculars. The observer is a lip-reader. You will enunciate clearly to avoid mistake."

"I understand," Traile said bitterly. "What are your conditions for reviving Eric Gordon?"

There was another pause.

"He is alive now," was the Crime Emperor's calm reply. "However, he is in a state of completely suspended animation, and I am the only one who can restore his normal functions. I warn you, if you attempt to use adrenalin or a similar preparation, it will kill him instantly."

"What are your conditions?" Traile repeated, this time harshly.

Again there was a pause, evidently while the lip-reader relayed his query.

"Your agreement to surrender yourself unarmed, alone, within an hour," answered Doctor Yen Sin. "The proper drug will then be delivered to any surgeon you designate. It is simply a matter of an intravenous injection."

"I agree," Traile said grimly. He waved Allen back as the agent frantically tried to protest.

He could hear the hiss of the Yellow Doctor's indrawn breath.

"I accept your word," Yen Sin spoke rapidly. "It is now almost eight o'clock. You will leave the building exactly at eight. A private car will draw up at the Forty-eighth Street entrance, and the chauffeur will address you as 'Mr. Scott'—in keeping with your present role. You will enter. He will take you to another location, where one of my agents will give you further instructions. If there is any attempt to have yourself followed, or any variation from this order, your young companion will never awaken."

"I have your sworn word that you'll send the drug?" Traile demanded.

"You have," said the Yellow Doctor, "on condition that you are my—guest—by nine o'clock."

THE MINIATURE radio became silent. As Traile stepped

out of the glare of light by the window, Allen made a helpless gesture.

"I think you've lost your senses. Eric couldn't be alive. Yen Sin's lying just to get you in his power."

Traile went past him, into the room where Eric Gordon lay. He knelt, felt for a heartbeat, then held a small mirror to Eric's nostrils.

"You see?" Allen said. "There's not a sign of life."

"That doesn't mean anything," Traile answered. "I've seen a Hindu miracle man go into a similar trance and let himself be buried alive for two weeks. But I never could learn what drug he took, or what they used to revive him."

"You can't go through with this," Allen persisted desperately, as Traile took off his shoulder harness. "It's suicide."

Traile looked down at Eric's pallid face while he put on his coat.

"If I don't, it will be murder." He turned abruptly and went into the other room. At the door he paused, looked sharply at the Federal man. "No rush call to your men, to try to have me followed. Until Eric is revived I'm holding you also to the promise I made Yen Sin."

Allen's face was a picture of misery.

"Damn it, I can't let you go, knowing what—"

"You'll help me by staying here with Eric," Traile broke in. "After eight o'clock, call the best doctor you know and have him waiting."

He put out his hand. Allen gripped it, swore helplessly. Traile went to the elevator. He rang, and the car came up. He went down to the lobby, was almost at the Forty-eighth Street side when he remembered about the X-ray film. He had intended to tell Allen. He hesitated, but already the clock was striking eight.

He turned and went on out. A long black car was sliding up to the curb. It was, he thought with grim humor, vaguely like a hearse.

CHAPTER 12
THE ROOM OF THE DOLLS

I N THE dimly-lighted chamber which contained the talking Buddha, a panel had silently opened. Doctor Yen Sin paused in the aperture, spoke in Mandarin dialect to someone in the passage behind him.

"I have finished with him. Prepare the scene as I directed earlier, so that it will make the proper impression upon our friends."

"*Tche*, Master," the other man answered hastily.

The Yellow Doctor stepped into the room, and the panel closed behind him. He paused, glanced impassively at the clock, then began to remove the long rubber gloves which covered his hands. There was blood on the tips, and in place of his usual embroidered robes he wore a jacket similar to a surgeon's operating gown, save that it was shorter and was decorated with silken braid.

He laid the gloves aside, was about to remove the surgical gown, when the eyes of the Buddha glowed with white light.

Impatiently, he touched a long-nailed finger to a button on the table before him.

"I ordered that all routine reports were to be received by Kang Fu."

"This is an emergency, Master," the half-caste's anxious voice came from the idol. "I believe the man Traile is trying to betray you in spite of his promise."

The Crime Emperor gazed fixedly at the Buddha.

"Condensed report," he directed.

"Followed instructions at his hotel and while being transferred," Kang Fu said hurriedly. "Met Agent Eighty-five at Position E, entered car with her, apparently not followed. No police or Federal men seen on arrival of car outside the Black Dragon, but on descending to the lower floor he was immediately noted by three men, one now identified as Department of Justice operative. The three men have stationed themselves in position to relay signals. One is watching Traile, another is on the balcony, and the third at a window on the rear court."

"Where are Traile and Agent Eighty-five now?" the Yellow Doctor inquired.

"Near the roulette table in the Lotus Room," replied the Eurasian. "Agent Eighty-five was signaled to delay until further instructions."

Doctor Yen Sin turned and looked at the diagram painted on the opposite wall.

"It is a simple problem." He rapidly gave instructions, adding: "Allow ten minutes for Group Seven to get placed. Also, make arrangements to escort Citizens Five and Eight by one of the other entrances instead of through the Black Dragon."

"Citizen Five has already been admitted," came the reply from the Buddha. "He arrived early, and was taken to the usual room."

"Very well, proceed with your orders," directed Doctor Yen Sin.

THE LIGHT faded from the eyes of the idol. The Crime Emperor gazed down with a thoughtful look on his saffron face. Then with sudden decision, he crossed to the Dictaphone under the painted diagram. He inserted a plug, and one of the lights on the diagram flickered.

"Advise Citizen Five that I will speak with him," Doctor Yen Sin said coldly.

"But, Master, he has not yet arrived," was the quick answer.

The Yellow Doctor stiffened.

"He was admitted some time ago, through Entrance Three?"

"Something must be wrong, Master," the unseen man replied in alarm. "The Frenchman, Lecoste, went to escort him here, twenty minutes ago, but they did not return. I wondered at his being so early—"

The word was broken as Yen Sin snatched the plug from its socket. With a look of rage, the Crime Emperor whirled to the Buddha. He jabbed a button, spoke fiercely in Chinese, then slid open the hidden panel and hurried into the passage. A few seconds later a similar panel opened in one side of a small octagonal room. The section which the Yellow Doctor had entered was almost in darkness. A partition had been built

125

The Burman killer came
hurtling down headfirst.

across the center of the room, almost touching the walls on both sides. Back of it was a heavy chair, placed so that the occupant could easily see through the special black glass in the

middle of the partition, and yet be invisible from the other side. A microphone and several switches were mounted on a small shelf just under the rectangular black glass.

Yen Sin hurriedly passed through the narrow space between the left side of the partition and the wall. A light shone down on the other half of the octagonal room, revealing three glass panels which formed a bay at the front. The panel at the left had been partly slid back into a niche in the wall. Beyond the three panels a long room with a table and chairs was visible. A ceremonial pedestal stood just inside the center panel.

After one furious glance at the opened section. Doctor Yen Sin turned swiftly toward the front of the partition. Directly under the rectangle of black glass was a cabinet about three feet square. It was almost filled with hideous-faced masculine dolls. There were two rows of them, all dressed in men's attire, like ugly little puppets in some wholly male farce.

On the upper shelf, between the third and fifth doll, was an empty space. Where the fourth puppet had been, two insulated wires had been neatly clipped. As the Yellow Doctor saw the space and the severed wires, a murderous flame blazed up in his tawny eyes. He went to the side of the partition, stepped back of it to where the microphone stood. One talonlike hand raked at a switch.

"Kang Fu!" he rasped out.

"Yes, Master!" came the frightened half-caste's answer.

"Warn all searching parties!" the Yellow Doctor snarled. "Citizen Five and Lecoste have stolen one of the dolls!"

IN THE softly-lighted Lotus Room, under the ornate restaurant known as the Black Dragon, Michael Traile stood coolly waiting. From the moment he had entered with Iris Vaughan, he had been aware of furtive movements among the group of

men and women who filled the room. The wooden-faced crou-
pier at the roulette table, a German by his appearance, was
watching him from the corner of his eye.

As another minute passed, Traile turned to the blonde girl
beside him.

"Since we are to await the Doctor's pleasure," he said carelessly, "we may as well sit down."

He motioned toward a divan, but Iris Vaughan, who had
been nervously watching the other end of the room, shook her
head.

"No, we are to go on now," she whispered. Her pretty face
was colorless under her rouge. Traile looked down at her, as he
followed into the hall.

"One would think you were to be the victim," he said iron-
ically.

Her luminous blue eyes, too bright from opium, took on a
certain hardness.

"It is not my fault if you choose to be a fool. You came here
of your own free will."

They had turned toward the right. Traile saw three or four
men near a door a few yards away. A dark-haired girl in a red
evening gown, with a light cloak thrown over her shoulders,
was just entering. She glanced around quickly, gave a start as
she glimpsed Traile.

It was Sonya Damitri.

For a fraction of a second, her black, mysterious eyes seemed
to be trying to convey some message. Then she hurried on into
the room. The men near the door closed about Traile as he

followed with Iris. His eyes swept quickly about the room. It appeared to be the office for the gambling establishment. A fat Chinese sat behind a desk, a benevolent smile on his face.

He was looking toward Sonya, who had turned to a large wardrobe cabinet at one side, when a muffled cry sounded—apparently from the wall behind the cabinet. In the same instant, the phone on the desk rang shrilly.

Before the Chinese could pick up the instrument, the doors of the cabinet burst open. Sonya gasped and stepped back. A man leaped out, a pair of brass knuckles on each hand. A small, bloody spike protruded from the center knuckle on each hand.

"Lecoste!" Sonya cried out in astonishment. "What are you—"

"Get out of my way!" rasped the Frenchman. He whirled toward the hall. The men near Traile sprang after him. The Frenchman struck viciously with the spiked knuckles. One man fell back with a shriek. Lecoste drove his left fist into another man's face. Suddenly the Chinese gave a screech of terror as a second man appeared from the passage back of the cabinet.

The light showed the rubber mask of a Gray Man. But it was not this which had brought that squeal of terror to the Oriental's lips. His slanting eyes were fixed on a hideous little doll the man carefully gripped in both hands. As Iris Vaughan saw the doll she, too, gave a cry of fear, then turned and fled.

Sonya had leaped back into one corner. The two remaining men struggling with Lecoste suddenly jumped for the hall. Holding the puppet vertically with both hands, the Gray Man stepped through the cabinet, made for the doorway. In his haste, he stumbled over the doorsill, fell headlong on the doll.

INSTANTLY, THERE was a flash of rainbow fire. As the weirdly-colored blaze leaped up, Traile threw himself back. A terrific heat swept out after him, then the room began to fill with the rainbow smoke.

The Gray Man's voice rose in a frightful scream, the same frenzied cry which Jim Stone had given before he died. Gasping for breath, Traile felt his way along the wall. Cool air from somewhere led him on. He reached the cabinet, vaguely glimpsed Sonya as she ran into the passage.

He quickly followed. She went down a flight of steps, vanished around a turn. Above the hissing of the Rainbow Death, and the clamor from beyond the office, Traile heard her give a stifled exclamation. He reached the bottom of the steps, saw a heavy door standing ajar. A Chinese lay dead nearby, two ugly wounds in temple and throat showing where Lecoste's knuckle-spikes had stabbed him.

There was a telephone in a small recess just inside the entry. The wires had been cut. Traile stepped over the dead man, looked swiftly along the passage. There was but a single light, and its glow was feeble. He could barely see the girl as she paused before the seemingly solid brick wall at the end. She reached up, pushed at a spot about the height of her shoulder. A section of the brickwork lifted like a gate, and she stepped through. The section descended quickly.

Traile ran to the end of the passage, felt around for the hidden release. One brick moved inward under his hasty pressure, and the gate slid up. He found himself in another passage, wider than the first. It led off into blackness. He listened intently, caught the sound of Sonya's swift footsteps from the dark. Brushing one hand along the wall to guide him, he followed as silently as possible.

The footsteps ceased and he halted immediately. From somewhere back of him, but at a distance, he could hear a commotion. Two shots made muffled reports, and he thought someone screamed.

Then, suddenly, light showed through a vertical crack ahead, as a door was slowly opened. He waited, unmoving. The slit widened into a rectangle, and he saw the girl's slender figure silhouetted in the opening. She looked back into the darkness, then hurried inside. Traile ran on tiptoe, caught the edge of the door as it started to close. In a second he was in the room.

Sonya's back was turned, and she seemed to be looking down in horror at something on a black table. Her figure screened it from Traile's view. He hastily glanced around. One look, and he knew he was in the torture chamber of Doctor Yen Sin.

Back in the gloom stood a darkened suit of armor, with a row of gas jets which could be turned upon it, after some luckless victim was placed inside. From a beam overhead hung a stained pair of saw-toothed leg irons, mute testimony to the manner in which some ill-fated wretch had been suspended in agony. A rack, an iron boot by a forge, and a score of other torture devices gave evidence to the horrors which had taken place within this chamber.

They were all ranged along one side of the room. The other wall was bare, and of an odd, shiny blackness. But Traile had only a moment to inspect it. For Sonya, after that horrified glance down at the table, was turning away. He was at her side in a flash, one hand raised to stop the cry he expected. Her red lips parted in amazement, but only a moan came.

"Are you mad?" she whispered. "Why didn't you escape when you had the chance, up there?"

He started to reply, then he saw the thing on the table. For a second, he thought he was looking again on the mutilated body of Peter Courtland. There, on a decorated black velvet pall, lay a corpse in evening clothes. Like Courtland's, his head had been cut off and sewed on again, backward. Two tall candles shone down on the distorted face of the dead man. And there between them was the Golden Skull!

TRAILE STARED in fascination at the gleaming metal face, while Sonya frantically tugged at his arm. Then he shook her off, took a quick step and bent over the corpse. It was only after a second glance that he recognized the agonized features of Merton Cloyd.

"You must get away," Sonya was saying wildly. "You should never have followed me."

Traile's lean face was cold.

"You know why I am here."

"You can never hope to capture him," she said hopelessly. "He is too well guarded."

Traile's dark eyes bored into her.

"I am not trying to capture Yen Sin. I came to save the man who unfortunately has fallen in love with you."

Astonishment filled her lovely eyes.

"But I don't—" She turned, with a suddenly frightened look.

At the same moment Traile thought he heard a faint scuffing from the black gloom of the torture chamber. As he wheeled for an anxious glance, Sonya gasped and seized his arm. But before she could pull him aside, there was a swishing sound from above.

Then a noose flashed down over their heads.

Traile caught desperately at the rope, but it was already tightening about their necks. Sonya was swiftly drawn against him, her white hands futilely clutching at the noose. He had a brief glimpse of a snarling brown face, where a dacoit had crawled out on the beam above. Then a sibilant voice spoke hurriedly, and through the door he had left open came the Yellow Doctor.

A look of disappointment shot over the Burmese's face. He kept the noose taut, but ceased his pull on the rope. Dr. Yen Sin calmly approached, a scalpel gleaming in one claw-like hand.

"You are a few minutes late, Mr. Traile—but since you have already broken our agreement, it is no matter."

"I've kept my word," Traile said, his voice thick from the pressure of the noose against his throat. "I could have escaped when that fire bomb went off."

The Yellow Doctor gave him a sneering smile.

"You are lying. I have already had a report. You followed Sonya through the secret entrance, thinking your agents were close behind you."

Sonya was struggling to widen the noose. She flung an angry look up at the dacoit.

"Clumsy fool!" she said in Hindustani. "I drew him straight under you. You did not have to catch me, too."

"It will be only a brief inconvenience," Doctor Yen Sin said smoothly. "Kang Fu will be here with help in a moment."

He had stopped close to Traile, the scalpel half-raised with a mocking significance.

"I am sorry to tell you, Mr. Traile, that your men have been intercepted."

Traile's face hardened.

"I obeyed your instructions to the letter. If I was followed, I know nothing of it."

The Crime Emperor smiled contemptuously.

"Lies will not help you now. You chose to break faith, and for that, your friend will die."

"I've surrendered myself," Traile retorted fiercely. "I demand that you send the drug to revive him."

Sonya Damitri twisted around, her great black eyes fixed on him with a strange expression. The dacoit up on the beam growled something in his throat. Doctor Yen Sin looked up sharply. In the same moment, light showed through the shiny black wall, disclosing that it was glass. Several figures were moving in the adjoining room. Desperation came over Traile as he saw Kang Fu and three of Yen Sin's killers. In another second, they would be entering through some secret door, and his last chance would be gone.

He stole a look toward the beam. The rope was pulled halfway around an upright to the ceiling, but the dacoit's eyes were on the Yellow Doctor, as he started to mutter something. Traile's

135

hands shot up and gripped the rope. Doctor Yen Sin sprang forward with a snarl. But that sudden, violent jerk had done its work.

PULLED OFF-BALANCE, the killer came plunging down headfirst. Yen Sin jumped back just in time. The hurtling form of the Burmese struck against his arm, and the scalpel fell from his hand. Then the dacoit thudded against the floor.

Traile's fingers were frantically widening the noose. As he cast it aside, the Yellow Doctor whirled to seize the knife. Traile crashed into him with a force that sent him back against the wall. Then he snatched up the scalpel and dashed for the door he had entered.

Sonya had sped out into the passage. Traile pulled at the door as he raced past, and it closed to a narrow slit. He was about to run in the direction from which he had come when the girl reappeared, caught at his arm.

"This way!" she whispered tensely.

He hastily followed her around a bend in the bricked tunnel. A connecting passage and two doors were dimly visible in the gloom.

"Take the second door," she said in a low tone. "Hide inside until I can come back."

Her voice rang out in a scream as he sprang into the darkness back of the opened door. He hauled the door almost shut, his pulses pounding as he heard the howls of Yen Sin's assassins in answer to Sonya's cry. In a few seconds there was a rush of feet, then a fierce jabbering of foreign voices.

"The left passage!" he heard Sonya tell them. The snarling

voices and sounds of running feet died away. Traile waited, then to his dismay the voice of the Crime Emperor came from only a few feet away. It was harsh with anger.

"If you had signaled from Entrance Three, he would have been caught before this could have happened."

"But the wires had been cut," Sonya protested in a voice that trembled. "And the rainbow fire had so frightened me—"

"Return and find Agent Eighty-five," the Yellow Doctor interrupted coldly. "I wish to question her, after the council meeting."

"I am sure she was not to blame," Sonya began, but Doctor Yen Sin peremptorily cut her short. Traile heard her move away, and after a moment he caught the soft footsteps of the Crime Emperor as he also departed.

He waited a minute, then cautiously opened the door. Indistinct sounds came from both directions outside. He looked back into his hiding place. It was a small room, littered with boxes—some empty, some of them unopened. He saw several trunks, two of them heavily roped. There was another door. He closed the one where he stood, moved across in the dark and tried the other. It was locked.

He stood in the dark, thinking intently. Yen Sin's killers might return and search this area when they failed to find him. It was doubtful that Sonya could get back in time to help him, and he was still not sure of her. At any moment, her dread of the Yellow Doctor might cause her to change her mind.

There was a slim chance that he could escape through the Black Dragon restaurant and return with a huge raiding party.

But it was the only way he could see to force Yen Sin to save Eric.

He started to open the door, holding the scalpel partly up his sleeve. Suddenly there was a click from behind him, and without further warning the other door swung open.

There stood one of the Gray Men!

CHAPTER 13
THE CULT OF
THE GOLDEN SKULL

AS THE light from the passage beyond fell on Traile, the Gray Man jumped back with an oath. His right hand plunged under his coat. Traile leaped, whirling the scalpel out of his sleeve. The Gray Man gave a cry of fear, threw himself aside. The blade scraped the edge of the door.

The Gray Man's hand reappeared with an automatic. Traile dropped the knife, seized the arm with the gun. A furious twist, and the weapon clattered to the floor. A muffled howl of pain came through the mouth-slit of the rubber mask. Then Traile's fist crashed on the other man's jaw. The Gray Man staggered, then came back with a snarl.

He swung wildly with his left. Traile shifted, landed an uppercut that sent the Gray Man reeling. Before he could recover, Traile snatched the mask away. The hate-filled eyes of Mark Bannister glared into his.

"I thought so!" Traile said grimly.

With a sudden lunge, Bannister dived at the gun. But Traile

had seen the purpose which tensed the millionaire's face. As Bannister's head went down, Traile swung with all his might. There was a crack like a half-muffled shot, and the millionaire sagged to the floor.

Traile bent over him, made sure that the man was not shamming. A hasty glance showed him that Bannister had been alone. The passage through which he had come ended with a dark glass door, of the type which he had seen before. The wall was decorated with red-and-gold circles. He closed the door, took out his cigarette lighter and lit it. With this to guide him, he cut the rope from one of the trunks. After a quick scrutiny, he removed Bannister's coat and tie, then bound the unconscious man. He substituted the millionaire's tie and coat for his own, pressed the adhesive edges of the rubber mask onto his face, and dropped Bannister's gun into his pocket. There was a signet ring on the millionaire's right middle finger. He slipped it onto his own.

A minute later he stepped out into the other passage. He had left the millionaire concealed as much as possible behind the boxes and trunks, and had improvised a gag. If luck were with him, he would be out of the secret base and on his way to phone for help before Bannister recovered or was found.

They were about the same height, and though Bannister was slightly heavier, the difference would not be easily noticed. In the left lapel of the millionaire's coat was a peculiar little ribbon which Traile suspected was a mark of identification. That and the gray mask should carry him through.

He was nearing the door to the torture chamber when he

saw a similar door about twenty feet farther on. It was open, and a stolid Chinese was following another of the Gray Men inside.

Traile paused, waiting for the door to be closed, but it remained open. He started on, intending to pass by hastily. But before he could reach it, the door to the torture chamber slid silently back, and the candlelight from the gruesome scene within fell squarely upon him.

The man who had opened the door was Kang Fu. He looked sharply at Traile, then glanced at the ribbon in his lapel. Then he turned and spoke toward the center of the gloomy room.

"Here he is now, Master."

The malignant face of the Yellow Doctor appeared in the candle glow. He beckoned imperiously to Traile.

"Come in, I have a final instruction for you."

TRAILE'S HEART sank. If he attempted to escape now, the alarm would be flashed before he could reach the entrance. He stepped inside, and Kang Fu closed the door. The Crime Emperor motioned the Eurasian out of earshot.

"I am anticipating trouble with Citizen Ten," he said in an ominous voice. "He is already in the Council Room. Go in and keep close watch on him until the others arrive. Do not forget your part. You, also, are supposed to be an unwilling member of the Empire."

"I know," Traile said in a harsh tone which closely resembled Bannister's voice.

The Yellow Doctor's weird eyes probed at his masked face.

"There is no occasion for fear about tonight's affair," he said impatiently, "if that is what troubles you. My men are searching, and Traile cannot escape. The deaths of Citizen Five and Lecoste have already been covered. Nothing can ruin our plans now."

Traile silently nodded. Doctor Yen Sin gestured to Kang Fu.

"When you have played the role of escort for Mr. Bannister, bring me one of the skull seals."

The half-caste looked at the gruesome display on the table, and Traile saw that the Golden Skull was gone.

"It has been returned to its proper place," the Crime Emperor said curtly. "I decided not to use it, as long as Traile knows the way into this room and is still at large."

At the mention of Traile's name, Kang Fu's sallow face took on an ugly expression. He looked significantly at the torture devices.

"When he is captured, Master, I hope you will let me take part in—"

"We will speak of that later," Doctor Yen Sin halted him. He waved a yellow claw, and the Eurasian opened the door. Traile followed him out into the passage. His hand closed around the butt of Bannister's gun as they started on, but his plan was abruptly thwarted. A searching party with flashlights was coming through the tunnel, and a burly Sikh was now standing guard at the secret gate in the brick wall.

The door through which the other Gray Man had gone was still open. Kang Fu stepped aside to let Traile precede him. Traile entered, a helpless feeling coming over him that some irresistible Fate had him in its hands. Then he thought of the

The Crime Emperor gave a baffled snarl and whirled from the wall of rainbow fire.

cold, white face of Eric Gordon, and the grim set came back to his jaw.

The room he had entered was not unlike the reception room of a small club, except that there was an Oriental touch to the furnishings. A thickset Chinese with horn-rimmed glasses began to open a record book on a desk, but after a second glance at Traile he stood up and drew aside a tapestry. A narrow corridor lay beyond. It was only about twelve feet in length, and as Traile neared the other end a solid door noiselessly opened.

It closed behind him as he went in. He looked back and saw that Kang Fu had disappeared. Then he heard a sound and glanced around. The Gray Man he had already seen was turning hastily. Traile guessed that he had been trying to peer through one of the sections of dark glass which formed the wall.

The man stared at him through the eye-slits of his rubber mask, then abruptly seated himself near the end of a long table. Traile saw that numbers had been neatly painted on the table, running in sequence from 1 to 16. The Gray Man had seated himself before the number 10.

TRAILE MOVED his eyes swiftly about the room. The walls on his right and left were composed of the peculiar black glass. Steel uprights divided the glass into sections six feet wide, and these were further divided into squares, so that they appeared like huge, dark French windows. He could see nothing beyond them.

At the other end of the room was a clear glass bay, formed of three heavy panels connected by metal frames and extending upward at least nine feet. This bay closed off the space behind it. Directly back of the center glass panel was a tall ceremonial pedestal. There was a round hole in its top.

A light was shining at an angle from the high ceiling. Its rays slanted down on the front of a wide partition behind the glass bay. In the middle of this partition, and just under a black rectangle, was an open-faced cabinet. Traile barely hid a start as he saw it. The cabinet was almost filled with ugly little puppets like the one which had caused the Rainbow Death.

There was something gruesomely suggestive about the faces of those hideous dolls. He stepped forward, moving carelessly, aware that sharp eyes were probably observing him from behind the dark glass walls. The Gray Man at the table jerked around as he passed.

"Be careful, you fool!" he said in a harsh whisper.

The door at the rear of the council room opened before Traile could reply. Two more of the masked men appeared. Kang Fu and two Chinese were briefly visible before the door closed. The newcomers stared at the cabinet, then silently took places at the table.

Traile sat down in front of the space marked 9. His chair was the first on the left, at the end near the glass bay. Citizen Ten was at his right, and the other men were seated across the table and farther down. The one at the space marked 6 looked again at the cabinet, and Traile saw him tremble.

The man's eyes seemed to be fixed on a puppet in the lower right-hand corner. It was a grotesque little figure, perhaps a foot high, with a bald, ugly head too large for its body. On the front of its tiny shirt was a red splotch, like a drop of blood, as though the puppet represented a man who had been stabbed.

The heads of the other dolls were also too large for their bodies, each being about the size of a man's clenched fist. Their lips and nostrils were sewn together with thread, and their eyes were tiny, vacant slits.

A wave of horror suddenly swept over Traile. He had been partly prepared; Allen's X-ray film had hinted at the fate of Meredith. But that frightful puppet show turned him sick and cold, as he realized the truth about those hideous dolls.

Each one bore the shrunken head of a murdered man!

Behind the rubber mask an icy perspiration bathed Traile's forehead. For a moment he thought that nausea would overcome him. But by a tremendous effort he controlled his sickened stomach.

A terrible fascination drew his eyes back to the puppets. He had seen shrunken heads before, in the Jivaro Indian country of South America. He had even witnessed the grim procedure which followed a head-hunting raid upon an enemy tribe. The slitting of the scalp from the hairline to the back of the neck… the removal of the skull… the sewing up of the scalp, the mouth, nostrils, and ears to retain the hot sand which kept the features intact while the empty head was boiled and toughened.

That had been bad enough, even in a savage atmosphere, with the victims as deadly as their killers. But this horrible display before him almost froze his blood.

THE REAR door opened again, and seven other Gray Men

entered. He saw each one look toward the shrunken heads, and in more than one man's hasty stare he read despair and horror.

Without a word, the masked men took their seats. Only their strained breathing broke the hush of the room. Traile watched them from behind his mask, saw their tight-clenched hands, saw their bodies go taut with fear. The tension swiftly increased.

From somewhere behind the glass bay came the sharp clash of a gong. Every man at the table jumped. As Traile jerked around he saw a dim light shine up through the hole in the tall, carved pedestal. Then, slowly, a gleaming object moved up into view.

It was the Golden Skull.

The jangling clash of the gong faded away. Traile gazed at the leering face of the skull, concealing a shudder as he thought of its grim secret. He started in spite of himself as an almost toneless voice came from those golden jaws.

"It is unfortunate that two more members of the *Chuen Gin Lou* will be absent—permanently."

The words were somewhat muffled by the thick glass, but Traile recognized the voice of Yen Sin.

"Citizen Five bribed an agent of the Invisible Empire," continued the voice from the Skull. "He attempted to withdraw from the *Chuen Gin Lou*, but met with a misfortune. His end was—colorful."

The man next to Traile shivered. Traile looked at the cabinet. He was close enough to see two severed wires where the death's-head doll had been fastened. It was obvious that an alarm had been disconnected. He remembered that Sonya had mentioned "rainbow fire." Evidently Doctor Yen Sin had placed a chemical bomb inside each puppet, arranged so that a slight impact or even tilting would set it off.

"The absence of Citizen Thirteen will be explained later—if necessary," the Yellow Doctor went on sibilantly. "But you have been summoned here for more important matters."

Traile heard a click, then one section of the dark glass swung back. A light went on in a vault, at the front of which was a large stack of engraved certificates.

"Citizen Seven, you will examine a few of the exhibits," directed the Invisible Emperor.

The Gray Man addressed went quickly to the vault. He picked up three or four of the certificates.

"They're bonds!" he exclaimed. "Good Heaven, there must be—" He broke off, hastily turned. "They're stolen! These four were stolen in the Union Trust robbery a year ago!"

"Your memory is excellent," came the mocking reply from the Skull. "You need not examine the rest. They are in the same category."

THREE OR four of the Gray Men gasped. Traile looked in amazement at the pile of bonds. There were, he knew from his reading of financial journals, almost a billion dollars' worth of stolen bonds in the United States. Normally only a small portion would ever be recovered or sold as legitimate bonds through dishonest brokerage houses. But it was plain that the Yellow Doctor had, through his vast criminal empire, drawn the larger part of the stolen securities from their various hiding places. The possibilities staggered his already taut brain.

"Details are unnecessary," he heard the silky voice of the Invisible Emperor. "The bonds will be equally divided, for sale through your banks and brokerage offices. It will be forty-eight hours before the truth is generally known. By that time—"

"But, my God!" cried Citizen Seven. "The losses have already been paid by the insurance companies. The market will have to absorb them again—it'll mean a panic worse than Twenty-nine!"

"I am not interested in the stock market of America," the hidden Chinese said coldly. "Here are my orders: As rapidly as the bonds are sold, they will be converted into foreign securities or jewels, as I direct, and these will be delivered to me by—"

"You're mad!" the man next to Traile broke in furiously. "It'll wreck the country—ruin us all—"

"Silence!" rasped the Invisible Emperor.

But Citizen Ten whirled frantically to the others.

"You damned fools, are you going to let him finish us? We'll be ruined—they'll jail us for—"

The crash of the unseen gong cut him off. He turned, shaking, looked toward the Golden Skull. There was a dead silence as the reverberations of the gong ceased. Then the Crime Emperor spoke in an icy tone.

"Perhaps you would rather go to the electric chair for—murder!"

"You tricked me into killing him!" the Gray Man said hoarsely. "By Heaven, I'll take my chances with the police!"

Traile had slid his hand into his pocket, was watching tensely. If the rest should rebel, there might be a chance....

"May I suggest," said the Invisible Emperor softly, "that you turn and look to your right?"

The Gray Man turned, went rigid. Diagonally across from the vault, another section of the dark glass had opened, revealing the torture room.

Though Traile had already seen the mutilated corpse, a chill ran down his spine. For beside the dead man's bier was a small guillotine. Its slanting blade was raised, and an ugly stain covered most of the surface. In the background stood several shadowy figures.

"Cloyd!" the Gray Man whispered as he saw the face of the corpse. He stumbled backward, dropped heavily into his chair. There was a sound like a faint mirthless laugh from the Golden Skull.

"I trust," said the Invisible Emperor, "there will be no further objections."

Citizen Ten buried his head in his hands. No one spoke. The pivoted black glass slowly began to close. It was almost shut when from the passage beyond the torture chamber came the unmistakable crack of a pistol shot.

Traile and several of the Gray Men leaped to their feet. A bright light flashed on in the torture chamber, as the waiting assassins whirled and ran for the passage. Then the Yellow Doctor's voice crackled from the amplifier back of the Skull.

"There is no cause for alarm. My men have obviously captured a certain spy who has been hiding in the base."

Traile was tightly gripping his gun. This might be a break....

There was a sound of fierce struggling, as the passage door

opened. A dozen of Yen Sin's killers appeared, dragging two men with them. Traile silently groaned as he recognized Bill Allen. His eyes shifted to the second man. Than he stood paralyzed.

It was Eric!

CHAPTER 14
THE END OF THE RAINBOW

IN THAT first moment, Traile almost doubted his senses. But the Yellow Doctor's men viciously shoved their captive into the lighted room and he saw that it was really Eric Gordon. The deathly pallor of the young Southerner's face had given way to an angry flush. He struggled for a second more, then gave up as he saw its futility.

Traile had instinctively sprung forward to help the two men. But even as he moved, he knew it was useless, and he transformed his hasty action into a threatening gesture. Bill Allen cursed him, and Eric gave him a savage glare.

Behind the group of dacoits and Chinese killers, three more figures appeared. Traile's eyes narrowed back of his mask slits as he saw Sonya with Iris Vaughan and Kang Fu. Then he realized that she could not know him, that she had not been able to return to the room where he had left Bannister.

Above the confusion and jabber of voices, an imperious command came from the Golden Skull.

"Kang Fu! Explain this, at once!"

The Eurasian gave Eric a half-frightened look.

"How this man recovered, I do not know, Master. He was leading the other one and a small party of Federal agents when Agent Eighty-five gave the alarm."

There was a short pause, and Traile guessed that the Yellow Doctor was looking at Iris Vaughan through the rectangle of dark glass. The blonde girl came forward nervously.

"I know nothing about it, either—I had just come in through Entrance Four when I saw them." She motioned to Sonya. "I was with her. We were unable to use the other entrance."

"What of the raiding party?" the Invisible Emperor demanded.

It was Kang Fu who answered.

"One of the men was killed. The others were shut out when we closed the emergency door. Group Five has been sent to take care of them."

"And you still have not found the man Traile?" came a harsh query from the Skull.

"No, Master, but it is impossible for him to escape," the half-caste replied hastily.

"Are you blind?" the Invisible Emperor said in a fierce voice. "This entire affair is a conspiracy. Traile must have known about the drug, and he simply pretended to agree to my conditions so he could discover the base. He must have some scheme to wreck our plans."

For just an instant, Traile caught a strange look in Sonya Damitri's eyes. And he knew, then, how Eric had been revived. But Kang Fu's next words snatched his mind from that brief, revealing thought.

"These two must know what Traile intends, Master. It should not take long to make them talk."

Before Yen Sin could answer, Traile wheeled toward the glass bay, which he knew shielded the Yellow Doctor.

"Let me handle them!" he said harshly. "I've a score to settle with both of them."

He thought Sonya gave a start, in spite of his careful imitation of the millionaire's grating voice. But Yen Sin's answer showed he had no suspicion.

"Very well. Kang Fu will assist you."

THE TIGHT band about Traile's heart relaxed. He nodded to the Eurasian. Kang Fu ordered the others to take out the captives. They were starting through the opening to the torture room when, without the slightest warning, the black section next to the vault whirled open on its pivots.

Then Mark Bannister plunged into the room.

There was a stifled exclamation from the Golden Skull, and Yen Sin's voice rose sharply.

"Kang Fu! Seize the man behind you!"

Traile had leaped back the instant he saw the millionaire. Kang Fu spun around, halted with a look of stupefaction. As Traile snatched the gun from his pocket, the half-caste frantically raised his own pistol.

Traile fired. Kang Fu crumpled to the floor, and Bannister tripped over him in his furious charge. One of the Gray Men clawed out at Traile's gun hand. Traile jumped sidewise, stiff-armed the other man.

In the sudden confusion, Eric had wrenched away from his

captors. He hurled himself down after the half-caste's pistol. A squealing Chinese dashed after him with a knife. Traile drilled the man through the head. Two of the Gray Men were almost on him. He slammed the gun across the nearer one's face. The rubber mask tore away, and he saw a bleeding gash. Before the second man could reach him, Traile hurdled a chair and jumped onto the table.

The second Gray Man dived at his legs. He lashed out, kicked the man squarely under the jaw. The Gray Man fell back with a strangled groan. Traile flung a look upward, crouched swiftly. Two dacoits were springing to drag him down. He leaped up with all his might, hooked one arm over the top of the center bay-panel.

Clutching hands caught at his feet. He kicked backward, felt the thud of his foot against flesh. His gun had slipped from his fingers as he grasped the top of the panel, pulled himself up with both hands.

Back of the partition, the Satanic face of the Yellow Doctor glared up at him. As he swung himself over the top, a gun blasted from the council room. The slug made a scar on the bulletproof panel, ricocheted up to the ceiling. Two more shots crashed against the glass as he dropped.

He struck beside the pedestal. Like a flash, the black rectangle was slid aside, and the snout of a peculiar weapon appeared. He threw himself flat. There was a twang, and a steel dart buried itself in the side of the pedestal.

As Yen Sin stepped back to recharge the gun, Traile sprang to his feet. The Crime Emperor stabbed a yellow talon at a button before him, and the right bay-panel swished back into a niche. Bannister and four of Yen Sin's killers darted toward the opening.

Traile whirled, snatched one of the death's-head dolls, and hurled it toward the onrushing men. A horrified look shot into Bannister's face as he saw the doll. He jumped back, threw his hand before his eyes.

There was a brilliant flash, an awful shriek, and the millionaire was lost in a blaze of rainbow fire. As Yen Sin ran toward the other side, Traile saw two more groups closing in. He turned desperately and jerked one after another of the deadly puppets from their wires. He saw it land near the pile of bonds, and another blaze up near the door to the torture room.

ALARM BELLS were clanging wildly above the hiss of the Rainbow Death and the screams of the dying men. Traile felt his way toward the right side of the bay, to the opening through which Yen Sin had fled.

The Yellow Doctor's voice was audible from across the council room. As Traile ran toward the spot, the rainbow-colored smoke billowed from a sudden draft. He saw three or four of the Gray Men dashing to the rear door. Eric was hastily drawing Sonya away from the flames. The girl swayed against him, almost overcome by the smoke.

From the direction of the torture chamber came a rattle of shots. Traile heard Allen bawl out something. He stumbled on toward the other side of the room. The pile of stolen bonds was blazing fiercely, and by the glare he caught sight of a yellow-robed figure only a few yards away. He leaped to bar the opening for which Doctor Yen Sin was making.

The Crime Emperor gave a baffled snarl, whirled to spring past the heap of blazing paper. The flames eddied out at him. He threw one hand before his eyes, staggered back into the vault. Then a wall of rainbow fire billowed across the entrance.

The heat forced Traile back. His feet struck Kang Fu's body, and as he tripped to his knees he saw part of a rainbow skeleton where Bannister had dropped. The draft sent the smoke whirling again, and he saw Allen and two of his men charge into the room, handkerchiefs held at their nostrils.

"Watch out!" Traile called huskily as they neared him. "Some of Yen Sin's killers may still be here."

The senior agent limped toward him, his mouth bleeding, and his clothes torn half from him.

"I think the damned rats are taking it on the lam," he said thickly through the handkerchief. "The other four squads finally got in through that restaurant."

Traile quickly pointed toward the blazing bonds.

"Keep your guns trained over there. Yen Sin was forced into that vault, and if the smoke hasn't stupefied him he'll try to make a break."

A few moments later Eric reappeared, but Sonya was not to be seen. Eric met his gaze firmly.

"I helped her escape, Michael."

Traile slowly nodded.

"I understand, old man. I hope she gets away."

Allen came over to them, stared through one of the open

bay panels at the Golden Skull. Traile saw the grimace which came to his face.

"Then you guessed what that X-ray was?"

The F.B.I. man grimly wagged his head.

"Yes, when Eric told me that Yen Sin had threatened to cut off his head and shrink it for a present to you. I doped it out then that Meredith's shrunken head was inside the Golden Skull. Poor old Stone must have made an X-ray of the skull at the last minute. Nobody thought to look at the machine, and later that forged paper must have been X-rayed on the same film."

"It was a fiendish idea," Traile muttered. "The original Golden Skull was probably only a symbol, but Yen Sin used this one to keep a merciless hold on the Gray Men. I suspect that he tricked a number of them into helping kill Meredith, perhaps by threat of torture. Those tiny marks we saw on the forehead are undoubtedly the signatures of the members of the cult."

THE TWO agents with Allen stared in astonishment at Traile's revelations. He peered toward the vault, went on hurriedly.

"After cutting off the ears, and mutilating the nose and lips, he simply plated the head with gold to hide what it really was and to preserve the signatures. That way, he had the corpus delicti and what amounted to a signed confession in form he could easily move from one place to another. Those other shrunken heads evidently served the same purpose for later members. If someone hadn't taken the real skull to Courtland's home instead of one of the seals, we'd probably never have known."

"Well, we'll know plenty when we get another X-ray and read those names," muttered Allen.

Traile's dark eyes were grave.

"We'd better forget the Gray Men, Allen. To publish the truth about this might wreck Wall Street—and the country. Better by far to drop the skull in that fire and destroy the heads later. After all, most of those poor wretches were driven by torture and blackmail, and tricked into those killings."

Allen looked fiercely toward the vault.

"I hope I'm there to see it when they strap Yen Sin in the chair!"

Traile shook his head.

"I'm afraid it's too late for that. The yellow butcher is probably roasted by now."

To his amazement, the voice of Yen Sin replied sonorously through the Golden Skull.

"I am sorry to disappoint you, Mr. Traile. The 'Yellow Butcher' is quite alive—as you may soon regret."

Traile stared down, speechless.

"Holy Moses!" Eric breathed. "He's evidently got away to some other part of the base."

Traile looked grimly at the now silent skull.

"That vault looked solid. But I was a fool not to suspect there was another entrance."

"We might still catch him!" grated Allen.

A briefly bitter smile came to Traile's lips.

"No, he wouldn't have mocked us if he hadn't already been safe." Then his eyes fell on the colored flames consuming the stolen bonds. "But there's one thing certain. He'll find no pot of gold at the end of that rainbow."

POPULAR PUBLICATIONS
HERO PULPS

LOOK FOR MORE SOON!

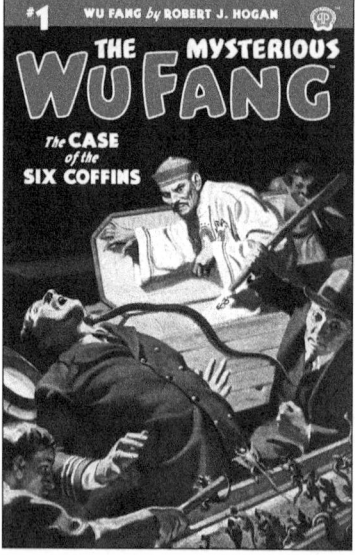